Kill Or Die

Ann Evans

Copyright © 2017 Ann Evans

The right of Ann Evans to be identified as the Author of the Work has been asserted by her in accordance Copyright, Designs and Patents Act 1988.

First published in 2017 by Bloodhound Books

Apart from any use permitted under UK copyright law, this publication may only be reproduced, stored, or transmitted, in any form, or by any means, with prior permission in writing of the publisher or, in the case of reprographic production, in accordance with the terms of licences issued by the Copyright Licensing Agency.

All characters in this publication are fictitious and any resemblance to real persons, living or dead, is purely coincidental.

www.bloodhoundbooks.com

Print ISBN-978-1-912175-14-7

I'd like to dedicate this book to Wayne, Angie and Debbie who have grown up with a mum who is constantly writing! Also for their 'other halves' Mel, George and Steve. For Jake too, who is old enough to read this book now. Love also to Megan, Brennan, Sam, Nathaniel, Anya and Ethen who aren't old enough to read it – yet.

A special thanks to Betsy, Fred and all the team at Bloodhound Books for taking a chance on me, and for all the help and support.

Chapter 1

The fog came down before midnight. Like a clammy grey blanket, it silently descended over the Warwickshire village of Old church, smothering the elegant black and white timber-framed houses lining Sycamore Drive. And, with the fog, came an oppressive dankness and a freezing damp.

A little after one am, the pale glow of a car's sidelights cut through the swirling mist. The car turned into the street, and coasted silently to the curb. The driver's caution, however, was not for fear of hitting anything in the claustrophobic gloom, but because he wanted his presence to go unnoticed.

Vincent Webb sat hunched over the wheel, making himself smaller, less visible, less memorable. If anyone was watching, which he doubted, better they didn't notice a big, blond good looking twenty-eight-year-old, sitting there; someone they could hardly forget. He needed to keep a low profile. Tonight, he needed to be invisible.

Making sure, he pulled a black woollen balaclava over his head. Slate blue eyes peered through the slit, focussing on the house opposite. The house he and his companion, Nash, were about to visit.

Vincent Webb glanced at Nash slouched in the passenger seat. He wasn't a pretty sight. Life had not been kind to Nash, and it showed. Scarred in a knife fight, and sewn back together by someone who didn't give a damn.

"This fog's a blessing, don't you think, Nash?" Vincent prided himself on his educated voice. It was mellow, cultivated. A radio-voice, some said. It held a certain charm women in particular warmed to. A voice that had talked him into beds, and out of tricky situations, on many occasions. Vincent Webb relied on three things – his charm, his good looks, and his resolute determination to never allow anyone to get one over on him.

He patted the scarred man on the arm. Vincent wore black leather gloves that went well with his black Italian leather trench coat. Nash wore black denim. "The fog, it's a gift from the gods. It conceals us. We're invisible. Who's going to remember us being here? No one. Because no one can see us. It's beautiful."

The thinner man rubbed a hand over the right side of his face, where the wounds from the knife attack, five years before, stood out angrily against his white, pock-marked skin.

"Hate the fog. Hate the cold. Gets into my face, y'know, seeps into my scars. Even these little pin holes, where that quack stitched me, they hurt like needles jabbing in this cold weather. My whole headaches. You've no idea, Vince. The cold kills me."

"Kills me, too, Nash, every time I have to look at your ugly mug." Vincent took the sting out of his words, by smiling behind his balaclava, making sure the smile touched his eyes. It was a skill he'd mastered over this last year since knowing Nash. He kept the smile in place behind the woollen mask, as if to pacify, like he was speaking to a child, or dumb animal, neither of which Nash was. And that was something Vincent had no intention of ever forgetting.

"How are we gonna know which house it is in this fog, Vince?" Nash's words spilled out on a build-up of saliva. Automatically, he wiped his arm across the misshapen mouth.

"Have faith, my friend. Have a little faith." There was no mistaking the house; Vincent had checked it out days earlier. He'd know the way blindfolded. He knew behind this barricade of Leylandii trees stood a fancy mock Tudor house, dripping with priceless antiques. And there was one old man guarding his hoard. He'd done his research. The old guy was a connoisseur. He knew the old man owned one collection of silverware worth two hundred thousand; his Chinese jade collection was worth a half million – and Vincent's contact in London had buyers waiting.

They sat in silence for a while, peering through the grimy window of the stolen car. There were no lights on in the house, at least none he could see through the fog and trees. But, he'd give it another few minutes, to be on the safe side.

He stretched his legs – or attempted to. Why the hell Nash had lifted this wreck, he didn't know. It stank of stale fags, and there was a spring sticking through his seat. They'd done the owners a favour nicking this heap of crap.

"Is this gonna be the big one, Vince," Nash mumbled, hugging his arms around his skinny frame for warmth. "Is this the job that's gonna make us rich? Coz this bloody cold weather cripples me. I need to get away, somewhere warm…"

"That's the idea, my friend," Vincent said, shutting him up, before he started whining on about his face again. Somehow, he kept the impatience out of his voice. The kid glove treatment was another trick he'd learnt when dealing with Nash. He was as touchy as hell about his appearance - which was understandable. The scar ran from the outer corner of his right eye, down to the lower edge of his lip. Pinholes ran down either side of it. The fight had happened when Nash was seventeen, and had left his face virtually sliced in half. The muscles were severed and destroyed, along with any thread of affection he'd ever had for his fellow mankind.

"He's loaded, right?"

"Like you wouldn't believe, my friend."

Vincent hadn't told Nash the extent of the old guy's wealth. No point doing that. He didn't want to risk Nash getting greedy. Anyway, Nash hadn't been the one who had devised and set up this job. *He* was the brains. Nash was merely the brawn.

"He'd better be," muttered Nash. "If I don't get into a warm climate soon, I'm gonna die. California, that's where I'm off to, once we've got enough dough. Gonna book myself into one of them clinics. Y'know, one of them plastic surgery places."

Vincent gave him the benefit of a reassuring wink. "They'll fix you up good as new, no sweat."

The unmarked side of Nash's face creased into a crooked smile, but because of his lack of muscle control, it turned into a sneer.

Vincent turned away.

"Yeah," said Nash, clasping and unclasping his woollen-gloved hands. "If they can turn old hags into raving beauties, they'll do me, no worries."

"Sure will," agreed Vincent, winding down the side window. Fog drifted in, smelling of smoke and November.

"Shut it, for Christ sakes," Nash whined. "It's cold enough with the window up."

Vincent did so, without argument. Not out of consideration or fear of Nash's mood, but because it was almost time.

"Just a few more minutes," he said. "Make sure the place stays in darkness, although I imagine he'll be well off into the Land of Nod by now."

"It don't worry me none if he's asleep or not," Nash slurred, his eyes coming alive with a spark of dark menace.

Vincent tried not to let it get to him. Although, sometimes, when Nash had that look, he seemed totally insane. It worried him, at times. Not that he'd ever let his fear show. That wouldn't do at all.

It had been down to his ability to hide his emotions that first landed him with Nash. He'd been relaxing in a pub, after a particularly good bit of business a year ago, when he'd spotted Nash sitting alone in a corner. He'd been trying to drink his beer, but it was slopping out of his misshapen mouth faster than it was going down his throat. It had turned Vincent's stomach. But, when he'd glanced at him, Vincent had managed to give him a friendly smile, and hide the revulsion.

Ten minutes later, a fight broke out, and some moron had come at him with a chair. Nash had stepped in and floored the man with a crushing blow to the back of his skull, sliding the lead cosh back into his jacket seconds later. He'd then hauled Vincent to his feet.

It wasn't until weeks later, and two successful armed robberies behind them, that Vincent had learned why Nash had taken a liking to him. He'd been the only person in years who hadn't beheld him with disgust.

And they say the Chinese are inscrutable.

"It really scares me though, Vince," Nash's whimpering broke through his thoughts.

"What? Some old boy, loaded, living alone and probably deaf as a post?"

"Not the job," said Nash, sucking and swallowing. "Plastic surgeons – the thought of being taken apart by some quack."

"Have a little trust, my friend. They aren't all butchers. Some are skilled craftsmen."

"Yeah! Like the one who did this?" he grumbled, clutching his face.

Vincent spoke softly, as if pacifying some cornered animal. "The doctor didn't do that. The doctor stitched you back together. Where would you have been, if he hadn't sewn you up? You'd still be in two halves – a split personality."

The half-smile contorted beyond any semblance of what a smile should be It wasn't in recognition of Vincent's attempt at humour, as he well knew. He'd heard the story of Nash's revenge, time and time again. In a macabre way, it sickened and impressed him – the fact Nash had mutilated the surgeon who had saved his life, because he'd left him ugly. And not only the surgeon, but his wife, too—worked on her with a nasty little Stanley knife.

One would think after hearing the details a couple of dozen times, it would lose its impact, but it didn't. Sometimes, Vincent wondered if Nash knew how it wound him up inside. He probably only harped on to keep him on his toes—a subtle warning of what he'd do if he ever was crossed.

He'd have to be careful how he split with Nash, when the time came, very careful.

"Could do with a fag," Nash said, pulling off his gloves, and rubbing his hands over his thighs.

"Have one, then," Vincent snapped, checking his watch again.

"You ever seen me smoke? Huh? Have you?"

"Steady on," Vincent said, patting the other man's knee. "No point in getting your knickers in a twist. If you need a fag, have one. Simple as that."

"Ever tried smoking, when you got no feeling in your face? I used to enjoy a fag. Used to like chewing gum, and all." His voice took on a bitter whinge, and his hands clenched into fists. "Used to enjoy eating and drinking, and screwing…"

He kicked out at the dashboard, and a CD jumped out of the player and landed in the console amongst empty fag packets and ash.

Vincent fished the CD out, wiped it down the side of the seat, and slotted it back in. The Beatles. He liked the Beatles. He'd play that when they were on their way back to the house – or hovel, rather. They'd have something to celebrate, by then.

He turned his attention to Nash. His voice was calm, in total control. "Just think, mate, after this job, and you get yourself off to sunnier climes, you'll be having as many ciggies as you want, and as many women. They're crazy about the English over in the States, especially those old birds."

"It had better happen, Vince. I gotta get somewhere warm. This cold is killing me."

Vincent adjusted his own gloves and balaclava. "Then, we'd better make sure nothing goes wrong. Ready?"

Nash's hand went instinctively to the inside of his denim jacket. The tools he carried made him look bulky, like he worked out regularly. Stripped naked, you could count his ribs.

A crooked, smile twisted his face as he pulled out a well-worn lump of lead, twelve inches long, and the circumference of a man's hand.

"Go easy with that," Vincent said, opening the car door, and stepping out into the freezing damp fog. "One of these days, you're going to kill somebody."

Nash sneered. "Yeah, you never know, Vince. Maybe I will."

Chapter 2

With a strangled sob, Julia Logan threw her mobile towards her open handbag on the sofa. She'd been on the verge of calling Ian, when the sound of a car door closing sent her running to the window again. But, Ian's car wasn't on the drive, as far as she could see. The fog seemed to be getting thicker by the minute. The sound must have travelled from across the street. Fog did that - distorted sounds, exaggerated them.

She let the heavy brocade curtain fall back into place, aware running to the window at every little sound was simply something to do. A break from watching the hands of the clock ticking round, reminding her Ian was late, Ian was somewhere else. Somewhere he ought not to be.

"Damn you, Ian Logan!" she exploded, checking the clock again. She had memorised every inch of its fancy gilt frame, knew the sound of its ticking and whirring. At times, she thought she'd pull it down from the wall, wrap it up, and send it to his blasted office. "There! You stare at it, hour after hour, night after night. No, you've forgotten all about time, haven't you, Ian? There's something more important on your mind now – *someone* more important," she shouted out to no one in particular.

She pressed her palms into her eyes, forcing back the tears. She wouldn't cry tonight. Tonight, she was going to be strong, stronger than she'd ever been.

She had made her decision two weeks ago. These last fourteen days had been her husband's probationary period, not that he'd known. It had been his last chance to give up the other woman. To come back to her, as the man she married. The man she loved – still loved, despite everything.

But, he had failed. Last night, it was the early hours of the morning before he came home, and then, it had been with some pathetic excuse of problems at work. He hadn't even the guts to tell her the truth. That would have been better than listening to his lies, pretending to accept them. Tonight, his excuse would be the fog. However, she wouldn't be there to hear his excuses. He had used his last chance.

Two packed suitcases were tucked inside her wardrobe. Last night, she had almost left him, but then, at the last moment, she had pushed the cases back into the wardrobe, and cried herself to sleep. Ian hadn't commented on her puffed eyes that morning before going to work. But, then, he couldn't even look her in the eye these days.

She ran upstairs, and dragged the suitcases out. They were heavy, but not as heavy as her heart. She took a final glance into her jewellery box, undecided whether to leave her wedding ring amongst all the other pieces she had no use for: some earrings, a couple of watches, an antique silver ring Benjamin Stanton from next door had given her. She skimmed her finger over it. The poor dear was almost housebound these days. She popped in sometimes to see how he was, and on Thursdays to do his shopping. The ring had been a token of his appreciation, probably quite valuable, but too showy for her liking. *Ian might like to give it to his fancy piece, whoever she was*, Julia thought bitterly, as she lugged the cases downstairs.

The freezing fog chilled her to the bone, as she squeezed them into the boot of her yellow Mini. She hoped it would start. It was a devil to start in the damp, and she regretted not putting it away in the garage earlier. Fingers crossed it wouldn't let her down tonight. Heart pounding, she went back indoors.

Already, the atmosphere of the house had changed. She had turned her back on him, and that blasted clock.

"There, go tick to yourself. I'm not listening anymore." But, her stomach tightened, and she knew she was making the biggest decision of her life.

Tears stung her eyes without warning. She wiped them away swiftly, decisively. Her mind was made up. There was no turning back. She had to leave now, this minute, before he returned, and found her on the verge of leaving. She couldn't cope with that.

She ran back upstairs, and into another bedroom. The hall light's glow fell across the narrow bed draped in pink netting, and the sleeping form laying amongst a heap of teddy bears. Julia gently brushed a fine golden curl back from her daughter's forehead. "Lucy, sweetheart, time to wake up."

The child stirred, her lips pouting cherub-like, before dragging the duvet over her ears.

Julia gently shook her. "Lucy, we have to go out. Wake up, sweetheart."

Lucy half-opened one blue eye and muttered, "School?"

"No, darling, but we have to go out. Please, Lucy, put a sweater on over your nightie, and slip your shoes on. I'll wrap you in a blanket, and you'll be lovely and snug in the car."

Lucy pulled a face. "I'm too tired. Don't want to go out."

Julia drew back the bedclothes, and eased her eight-year-old out of bed.

The child flopped awkwardly, head on her knees, grumbling. "Where we going, anyway?"

"Just to Aunty Steph's."

Groaning and straightening up, the child rubbed her eyes. "What about school? Miss Carter is picking Mary and Joseph tomorrow, and I want to be Mary or the Angel Gabriel."

Julia dragged a sweater over her daughter's head, hoping her sister wouldn't object to them turning up on her doorstep in the middle of the night. She hadn't even hinted to Steph her marriage was in trouble. She was going to be stunned.

Julia tried to keep focussed. "We'll still get you to school, Lucy, only we'll be staying at Aunty Steph's for a while. That'll be nice, won't it?"

"Suppose so," Lucy murmured, flopping back on her bed, eyes closed.

Julia dragged her upright again, easing her feet into shoes. "The minute we're in the car, you can go straight back to sleep, promise, only hurry, love, and help a bit, will you? You're as floppy as a rag doll."

Lucy stretched backwards to grab a threadbare teddy that had been Julia's when she was little. It pleased her to know it was her daughter's favourite, as it had been hers.

"Can I take Mister Brown?"

"Naturally we're taking Mister Brown. You don't think we'd forget him, do you?" She wrapped a blanket around her. "There, all set!"

Keeping an arm around her daughter's shoulders, in case she tripped over the trailing blanket, they went downstairs. And although Julia's smile remained fixed for Lucy's sake, inside, she was grieving. *Oh, Ian, come home now, see what you're doing to us.*

But, all was silent, except for the sound of a dog barking. It sounded like Bessie, Benjamin's collie.

On the third stair from the bottom, Lucy stopped abruptly. "Where's Daddy?"

Julia's eyes fluttered shut for a second, then taking a deep breath, she said, "Daddy isn't coming to Aunty Steph's. It's you, me, and Mister Brown. Daddy is staying here for a while."

The child's face crumpled. "Why?"

Julia blinked, and swallowed the lump in her throat. "I'll explain in the morning. Not tonight, please, Lucy."

"But, I want to say goodbye to him."

"He's not in," Julia said tightly, the bitterness in her voice startling them both. More softly, she added, "Daddy is still at work. Lucy, please, we have to hurry."

The child remained stubbornly on the third step. Intelligent blue eyes fixed on Julia's tear glistening ones. Solemnly, she asked, "Are you leaving my daddy?"

A sob gurgled in Julia's throat, and she took in her daughter's face. She was so like her father, it hurt to look at her at that moment they both had the deepest of blue eyes, and a way of looking directly at you, as if reading your thoughts. Although, it had been a while since Ian had looked into her eyes. These days, he spent more time avoiding them. "Lucy, I have to. For a while anyway, until…"

The child stamped her foot. "No! I don't want to. He'll be sad, if we go away."

"It's fine, darling. Please, we need to go."

Lucy turned troubled eyes towards her. "Don't you love him anymore?"

"Of course I do," Julia said, as if the thought was ridiculous.

"Doesn't he love me anymore, then?"

Julia hugged her fiercely. "Don't be silly. Of course he loves you."

"Does he know we're going to Aunty Steph's?"

Julia could see a hundred and one questions flying through her daughter's mind. With a defeated sigh, she shook her head. "No, love, he doesn't know."

The look on Lucy's face said she'd already guessed that. "Can I write him a letter?

Julia's eyes fluttered shut, the effort of holding back the tears physically hurt. She nodded.

Throwing off her blanket, Lucy raced back upstairs. Julia picked it up, and leaned against the wall, hugging the blanket to her chest, listening to the clock whirring and ticking. Benjamin's dog had stopped her barking, for which she was glad. She hoped the old man was all right. Bessie didn't usually bark, unless someone came to the door. Normally, she would check, or at least phone him. But, tonight, she needed to get away, now.

The solemn look on Lucy's little face, as she reappeared at the top of the stairs, banished all thoughts except the misery of what was happening to them. With the teddy tucked under her arm, Lucy descended gravely. Reaching the bottom, she wrapped the blanket around herself, and walked to the front door.

"Have you written your letter?" Julia asked softly, and as her daughter nodded, asked, "And may I ask what you wrote?"

Lucy said nothing, but mutely shook her head.

With a sigh, and a last look around her, Julia grabbed her car keys, and opened the front door. Even before she had stepped out into the freezing fog, she shivered.

Chapter 3

Benjamin Stanton eased himself halfway out of his bed. Fumbling for his spectacles, he clicked on the bedside lamp. It was an Edwardian lamp, and probably one of the newest pieces of furniture in his home. Like everything around him, it told a story; it had a history. Its soft glow illuminated his bedroom, and he saw his ageing rough collie, with her nose pressed up against the bedroom door, barking to be let out.

"Bessie, why did you have to wake me, hey? I was having such a nice dream. What's all this barking, anyway?"

Bess cocked her head, with pleading eyes, then, turned back to the door, and carried on barking.

"All right, wait till I get myself together. What's the matter? Need to pee? I told you to go before we came to bed, fog or no fog."

He pushed back the heavy eiderdown, and eased himself around to sit on the edge of his bed. He reached for his walking stick. His joints ached. He and Bessie were a pair, fit for the knackers' yard, and nothing else.

"Your bladder isn't what it used to be, is it, girl? Like mine. Well, keep your hair on, I'm being as quick as I can. You know, I was dreaming about my mother. Funny that, to dream about her after so long. You'd have liked her, Bess. She was a real softy with dogs. She'd have loved you."

He dragged on his robe, and shoved his feet into worn carpet slippers, as he spoke. Then, steadying himself, he shuffled to the door. The moment he turned the handle, Bessie's head was around the door, forcing it wide with her body and out of Benjamin's hands. She flew down the stairs, her paws barely touching the stair carpet, the way she used to when she was a pup.

Benjamin shuffled to the top stair, and gripped the banister. Bessie had skidded to a halt by the closed lounge door. She crouched with her nose to the bottom of it, her barking only broken by a deep throaty growl. Benjamin descended slowly, he was going to need a stair lift, if he got any shakier on his feet. "Bess, old girl, what the dickens has got into you... Bess?"

A white foam was gathering on Bessie's black gums by the time he reached her, and he felt the hairs on the back of his neck prickle. This wasn't Bessie needing to pee. This was bad. Heart pounding, he backed away from the door, clutching his walking stick, and feeling behind him for the telephone on the hall table. Before he could pick it up, the door sprang open.

At first, Benjamin thought Bessie had managed to turn the handle, as she pawed and scratched, until he saw his dog recoil backwards, lips drawn fully back to reveal her teeth. *Beautiful teeth*, Benjamin thought for a moment. But, the sound she made was like nothing he had ever heard his beloved companion make, in all their years together. Not a growl, more a rattle coming from deep down in her chest.

"Bess…"

A figure appeared from the lounge. A tall thin figure, all in black, face hidden behind a black mask. He could see eyes, though, through a slit in the mask. Manic, sunken eyes. Then, Bessie sprang, and those eyes screwed up in pain as her teeth latched on to his forearm. She hung there, legs dangling off the ground, swinging by her beautiful teeth from his arm, as he screamed and shrieked like a stuck pig.

Her sable and white fur was becoming tarnished by blood, more dripped onto the Persian carpet violating the pattern. Benjamin lifted his walking stick in defence, as a long piece of metal fell from the intruder's hand, and clattered to the floor.

He staggered to the phone, and with the receiver clutched in his shaking hand, he was suddenly overshadowed by someone towering over him. Someone else, dressed in black leather. The smell of it filled his senses. This one had only his eyes visible, like the one shrieking in the doorway. But, these weren't manic, pain filled eyes. These were wide, calculating eyes—pale, and filled with hate and anger. His arm was raised. That same length of iron was now being held above his head. It was lead, Benjamin could recognise any sort of metal. It even had a kind of smell. Only the smell of leather was uppermost now.

He had no time to cry out. In one swift, violent movement, the arm came down, and Benjamin felt himself sinking slowly, dropping to his knees. His own face, now streaked with blood reflecting back from every single silver button of the black leather trench coat, until he tasted carpet on his lips.

Benjamin's last thought was Bessie had stopped her snarling, too.

Chapter 4

Vincent stared down at the crumpled frail little man at his feet. Bile rose in his throat, and a burning fury tightened his stomach. Nash, the useless lump of crap, was slumped in the doorway, blood oozing from the rip in his jacket, and dripping from his sleeve.

"This was your job!" Vincent raged. "I did your fucking job."

"I'm bleeding Vince, my arm…"

"Stuff your arm!" Vincent snarled, stepping over the half-dead dog, and snatching a handful of Nash's jacket collar, twisting it around his fist. He dragged him to his feet. "You were too slow, too fucking slow! You do the shitty work. Not me. I shouldn't have done that. It's your job, not fucking mine!"

"Think it's got an artery. Do something, mate. Don't let me bleed to death."

"You're not going to bleed to death," Vincent snarled, wishing he would do just that. He loosened his grip, sickened to find Nash's blood all over him. "Grab a fucking bag, and follow me. We aren't quitting now."

Slowly, Nash slid down the wall, until he sat, splayed out, by the dog.

Vincent kicked out at the slumped form. "Get up. We can't hang about."

"Can't. Feel faint, Vince… Vince, help me, mate. Do something, please, Vince."

Vincent glared down at the pathetic figure crumpled on the floor, and pondered the pros and cons of actually leaving him to bleed to death. If he could be sure Nash would croak, before the coppers came, he'd shoot now. Only it would be his luck for

Nash to be still alive and squawking, when they got here. And it wasn't the prospect of Nash pointing the finger that bothered him. Worse was the thought of Nash looking for revenge at being left to take the rap. If he could carve up the surgeon who saved his life – and his missus, because he didn't do a pretty job, then God help anyone who deliberately crossed him.

With no alternative, Vincent grabbed Nash under the armpits, and hauled him to his feet. "Stay up. I'm not carrying you."

Nash wedged himself between the door posts. "It's gonna need stitching, get me to a hospital quick, mate. I can feel myself going."

Vincent swore under his breath, knowing if he wasn't going to do a runner, he'd have to help him. Cursing, he took off his trouser belt, and applied it in what he hoped was a tourniquet around Nash's upper arm. Then, snatching a lace cloth from the hall table, he bundled it against the rip in Nash's sleeve, where the blood was pumping from. "Press as hard as you can."

Nash's eyes were shut, his head flopped back against the wall. "Feel faint."

"You're bound to," Vincent said, knowing Nash would remember his treatment of him, if he didn't croak. "Didn't think a scrawny little runt like you had that much blood in him in the first place."

"Fainted at school once, in assembly," Nash mumbled, as Vincent tightened the tourniquet. "Teacher thought I was faking it, and left me there. Made everyone step over me. I came to, everyone gone, except for the Head, nasty bugger." He half-opened his eyes. "You're me mate though, Vince. Knew you wouldn't leave me."

"Yeah, yeah, save it, will you," Vincent muttered going into the kitchen to grab a couple of grubby tea towels. He tied them around the wound. "Keep your arm up, and the belt tight."

"Feel sick…"

"You aren't the only one," said Vincent, stepping over the old man, and running upstairs three at a time. "I'll do the bedrooms, you stay on your feet."

Systematically, Vincent went through each room, ransacking, looting, wrapping precious pottery into pillow cases and towelling. The antique silver collection filled an entire holdall. His excitement began to rise; the old man was loaded. This was the big one, all right.

He'd buy a decent car, nothing too flashy, something that would impress the ladies. It was one thing nicking a vehicle, only it was never your own. You couldn't ponce around in it, picking up women. No, he'd get himself off to a plush car showroom, take a few test runs. See them stuck up salesmen falling over themselves to serve him.

He headed back to the stairs, but his body jerked violently, as he looked down at the carnage in the hall. His throat gagged. Too much blood. A dead old man, a half-dead dog, both slain by his own hand. That's what incensed him. That was Nash's job. *What the hell did he think he kept him for? Not his company and good looks, for Christ sakes.*

The holdalls were heavy, and he lugged them downstairs, avoiding looking at the mess. Dumping the bags at Nash's feet, he went through to another room, a study, avoiding Nash's weak attempt to hold onto him. He worked swiftly, methodically, taking everything he could carry. Satisfied, he went back into the hall, gathered up all the bulging holdalls, and dumped them in the kitchen by the back door. He went back for Nash.

"Out the back, and keep the noise down."

The thinner man staggered, as Vincent pushed him out into the night. Vincent hung back. If the police had been called, they'd pounce on Nash first. He waited.

"Where you gone, Vince?" Nash's voice drifted through the fog.

"Shut it," he breathed, quickly following him, in case the idiot started yelling even louder. He closed the door with its shattered lock that had been so easy to force. If they hadn't been detected, then the longer they had to get away, before anybody realised something was up, the better.

"Get me to a hospital, Vince. Me arm's killing me."

"No hospitals," Vincent whispered, as they reached the car.

Nash shot him a frantic look. "But, I need fixing up. I won't grass. I'll say I was bitten by a stray dog. You don't have to come in with me. Just drop me off."

"I said, no hospitals."

Nash's pulled his balaclava off, his face twisted pathetically. "But, I gotta get this bleeding stopped, and I need one of them tetanus jabs. Ain't had one since me face got done."

Vincent opened the passenger door. "Get in, and stop harping on, will you?"

For a moment, Nash hesitated, and then, with a pained look, he slumped into the seat. Vincent clicked the door shut, and moved silently around to the driver's side. Once in, he buckled up his seatbelt, and turned the ignition key. The engine wrestled into life.

Nash slumped against him, saliva dribbling from the corner of his mouth. "Vince, please…"

"We can't take that chance, Nash," Vincent said, soothing him with his silky voice. "There'd be too many questions. You don't want to end up behind bars, do you? There aren't many plastic surgeons in prison, are there? Now, relax, and we'll put some antiseptic on it when we get back, and I'll bandage you up good and proper." He forced himself to look into Nash's eyes, and smile reassuringly. "You'll be as good as new again by tomorrow. Now, then, fancy a little Beatles' music?"

Nash closed his eyes. "Sure, Vince, mate, if you say so."

He pressed the 'play' button, slammed the car into gear, and stamped hard on the accelerator.

They had gone ten yards, before Vincent thought to switch on the headlights. As he flicked the switch, another vehicle materialised in the pale beam of light, pulling out of the next driveway. A yellow Mini.

His reactions were swift. He jabbed his foot hard down on the brakes, so the impact was nothing more than a scratch of metal and a tinkling of broken indicator light. But, for Nash, the sudden stop sent him catapulting forward into the windscreen. His forehead hit the toughened glass so hard, it shattered, and then, he whiplashed back into his seat.

Vincent stared through the blood splattered windscreen at the occupants of the Mini. A woman and a kid.

Witnesses.

Chapter 5

The car's headlights came out of nowhere, as Julia pulled out of her drive. She instinctively tried to swerve, but there was no avoiding the impact. It was slight, a faint tinkling of glass breaking – a sidelight or indicator light. In the back, Lucy buckled into her seat, cried out in fright.

Through the fog, Julia distinctively saw the driver brace his arms against the steering wheel, but his passenger shot forward, cracking his head against the windscreen so hard a circular cobweb effect of blood-smeared shattered glass instantly appeared, before he ricocheted back into his seat.

"God! That must have hurt. Stay here, Lucy. He might need an ambulance."

She got out, heart thumping, and dashed to the other car's passenger door. She was aware of the driver getting out, and walking around the back of his car towards her. He was tall, taller than Ian, and he was five eleven. This man was broad shouldered, too, and dressed all in black, like a large shadow she was only barely aware off, as she focussed on the passenger. He didn't seem to have moved since ricocheting back into his seat. She hoped to God he wasn't seriously injured.

"Shall I call an ambulance? I think your passenger is hu…"

Her question was left hanging in the air, as Julia realised she couldn't make out the driver's face, because he was wearing a woollen balaclava. Something stirred in the pit of her stomach. A slight warning. She ignored it. It was a horrible night. *Why wouldn't someone wear a balaclava?* What mattered was the passenger wasn't moving. *Was he unconscious? Dead?* God, she hoped not.

She went to open the passenger door when an arm, clad in black leather, was thrust in front of her, shoving her hand aside, and yanking open the passenger door. The thick smell of leather filled her senses, as he crowded over her.

"He couldn't have been wearing his seat belt..." she tried to say, but then the driver spoke.

"Nash, get your arse out of there."

Julia shot the man a sharp look, thinking how awful to snap out an order to someone who'd hit their head against a windscreen. Through the slit in the balaclava, his pale blue eyes were luminous – and cold.

The passenger looked to be in his mid-twenties, and horribly disfigured on one side of his face. He groaned, and slumped forward, his head almost in his lap.

"He needs help. My mobile's in my bag. I'll..." A leather gloved hand clamped suddenly and roughly around her mouth and nose, and she felt the terrifying feeling of suffocation. Frantically, she struggled against him, writhing, twisting, trying to kick back at his legs to scrape her heels down his shins. Desperately aware she couldn't breathe, she clawed at his hand, but she was being lifted bodily off the ground, and carried back to her own car. He bundled her into her driving seat.

"Shut it! One sound, and the kid dies, understand?" His eyes locked onto hers, glittering with menace.

"Mummy..." Lucy's whimpering voice reached her.

Everything was starting to swim before her eyes. His fingers dug into her face, the hand was locked rigidly in place. He peered past her, toward Lucy in the back. His voice took on a smoother tone, but the words were as deadly. "Be quiet, little girl, or your mummy dies. Do you understand?"

He leaned further into the car, squeezing his large bulk between Julia and the steering wheel, immobilising and smothering her.

Blood was pounding in her ears. She caught a glimpse of herself in the interior mirror, and saw her terrified bulging eyes. The car dipped, as someone got into the back seat next to Lucy, and the black gloved hand sprang away from her face. She gulped in the cold foggy air in big, desperate lungfuls.

Lucy cried out, then went instantly silent, as if someone's hand was over her mouth too.

"Don't hurt her!" she gasped. "Please, don't! She's only a child."

The leather-coated man peeled away from her, took his bulk, and his stench of leather away from her to stand by her open door. She spun around to her daughter, and saw to her relief no one was smothering her. But, the child sat rigid, her eyes huge with terror. Beside her, sat the injured man. He was slumped against Lucy, blood trickling in narrow gullies down his face. She saw he had another injury, as a belt had been fastened tight around his upper arm, and there was a pool of blood in his lap.

The man in black leather stooped down to speak to her. He spoke softly now, his voice little more than a whisper.

"My good friend, Nash, is now sitting beside your daughter. If you make any sound, hit the horn, or do anything rash, he will smash her pretty little skull in. Do you understand?"

Julia nodded, her eyes fixed on his through the slit in his mask. His pupils were dilated, as if highly excited, they terrified her.

"What you will do is drive," he instructed. "You will follow my car, which I shall drive. When I stop, you will pull in behind me. We will commandeer your little car, and you will be free to find your way home. Do you understand me?"

Julia nodded again, wanting to vomit.

He backed off steadily, his head inclined to one side, gauging her reaction. His finger pointed at her, like someone warning their dog to stay.

She didn't move, didn't disobey. There was no way she dared, with his accomplice sitting next to Lucy. She didn't know what this pair were up to, or what they were capable of. And she couldn't risk putting Lucy's life in danger by trying something heroic. So, she sat quietly, gripping the steering wheel with trembling hands, and watched him return to his car, reverse and pull around them, his eyes not wavering from hers for an instant.

"Follow him," the man in the back seat said. His voice was slurred.

Julia put her car into gear, and followed his tail lights through the fog, away from home, trapped in a nightmare of her own making.

Chapter 6

"I'll say you raped me!"

Ignoring her outburst, Ian Logan disentangled himself from Shelley de Main's arms, and swung his long legs off her bed. He pulled on his trousers, dressing quickly. Not that they'd done anything – not tonight, at any rate. He slipped his tie into his jacket pocket. Julia wouldn't expect him to have been working this late, and to come home still wearing his tie. He left the top button of his shirt undone, too, and pulled on his jacket. Catching sight of himself in Shelley's wardrobe mirror, he averted his eyes, not liking what he saw. Guilt. His face was riddled with it.

His gaze shifted back to Shelley. She lay sprawled across red satin sheets in what he guessed was supposed to be a seductive pose. She was naked beneath a short flimsy negligee, which was how she always dressed for him, when they were alone. Stockings, suspenders, Basques, see-through blouses – the whole sexy mistress stuff, which had excited him, at first, months ago. Only now, as she lay there, with her black hair spread out around her painted face on the pillow like a satanic halo, she reminded him of a plump Venus de Milo painting.

"I will, you know," she purred, the look in her green eyes fluctuating between mischief and actual warning. "If you say another word about us finishing, I shall scream rape. I'll scream it from the rooftops."

There was a knot in his stomach, as if the supper they had shared had gone down whole. "No one gets raped three times a week for four months, Shelley, not even you."

She raised herself from her bed, slipping on a robe equally as sheer, and floated open, as she glided towards him. She had a sultry walk, as if she'd seen how it was supposed to be done, and carried the whole sex goddess thing off to the letter. What a bloody fool he'd been, to have fallen for it.

She had a kind of beauty, he supposed; a faded beauty, which was certainly only skin deep. She was a woman still hanging on desperately to her youth. But, the silky fabric she draped herself in only served to contrast unkindly against her mottled skin.

Standing close to him, so her perfume swamped him, she slid her arms around his neck, stretching on tip-toe to kiss him. Not so long ago, the feel of her body against his had excited him. Now, it left him cold. It left him wishing he was home with Julia. This affair should never have happened.

"I'll say this was the first time," Shelley said huskily, looking up into his face. "I'll say you followed me home, talked your way in, and raped me."

Ian prised her hands apart, and stepped back. "Not much evidence of a struggle. Besides, I wouldn't make much of a rapist, would I?"

"You're tired, you work too hard. Come back to bed, Ian, and stop all of this silly talk of us finishing. You keep threatening, but you know you don't mean it. You've got a conscience, that's all. Sweetie, come on, let's go back to bed, and try again."

His eyes closed briefly, wearily. *Why the hell had he got himself tangled up with her?* It had been a massive mistake. "Shelley, we need to cool it…"

"I'm not listening," she sang dismissively, coiling around him again. "You couldn't live without me now. You love the excitement, the danger of being found out. The wickedness of it – and you know it."

He took a deep breath. He'd been along this track before. Only trying to break with Shelley was like beating his head against a brick wall. "It has to end, Shelley. I'm sorry. I'm really sorry. I never meant for anyone to get hurt."

"No one is getting hurt. We're having fun. It's not a problem. I don't want to break your marriage up. My God, I've got one husband. I don't want another."

"I'm hurting my wife," Ian said, setting her aside. Julia was no fool. She must have smelled Shelley's perfume on his clothes from all these late nights. He was an idiot to have thought he was fooling anyone, let alone a woman as smart as his wife.

Stupidly, it had started with an argument. He and Julia had had a blazing row, and he'd still been smarting by the time he reached work. Shelley had been there, pouring balm on his injured ego. *What a damn fool.* He'd walked straight into her clutches.

He'd always known she fancied him. She'd been flirting with him for as long as he'd known her, which had to be a year now. She was ten or twelve years older than him, and sexy in a tarty way. He'd been easy meat that morning – and for many mornings and evenings ever since.

She was clinging to him again, her breasts crushed against his chest, her hands stroking him. He pulled away, holding her at arm's length. "Shelley, I'm serious. This stops, now, this minute. We're both married. You don't really want to break up with your husband, and I certainly don't want to lose Julia and my daughter."

Her eyes narrowed, her pout deepened. "You should have thought about that before you fucked me."

"Alright! I know, and if I could turn back the clock, I would."

Her eyes grew moist. Any second now, she would turn on the tears, and he'd relent, like every other time he'd tried to break up with her.

Not tonight, though. Tonight, he wasn't going to back down. This whole affair was crazy; he didn't love Shelley; it was just sex. And, until all this started, he and Julia had a good sex life. It had deteriorated these last few months. He knew he'd used that as a reason to mess about with Shelley. Although, there hadn't been a minute when he hadn't felt riddled with guilt.

It had taken him four months to come to his senses. But, tonight, he knew this was the end for him and Shelley. And he was desperate to get away and back to Julia. If she did know he'd been having an affair, she was saying nothing, in the hope it would blow over. Well, tonight, it was well and truly over. He wouldn't let her down again.

True to form, Shelley's eyes filled with tears. "Ian, I couldn't bear it if we stopped seeing each other. How could we work together, after all we've been through?"

"We'll manage, and if we can't, I'll hand my notice in."

Her tears dried instantly, a harsh disbelieving look hardened her face. "Oh, yes, I'm sure. I can see you giving up your job."

"If it's impossible to work under the same roof, then, one of us will have to. And, as I started this whole thing, it's only fair I'm the one who goes."

"And what would you tell your wife?" she asked scathingly. "Won't she think it odd, seeing as you've been putting in all these long hours?"

"That will be my excuse, then. It's too much. I'm being put on," Ian answered, taking his overcoat from the back of a chair.

"Oh, you're so smart."

"Not smart enough, or I'd never had started this in the first place…"

The stinging sensation of her hand against his cheek came suddenly and harshly. The slap shocked him for a second. And, then, he saw it for what it was. The final word of a play. The end. No more. This sordid interlude was over. Without a word, he walked to the door.

"Don't you dare turn your back on me, Ian Logan," she screamed, reaching the door before him, and pressing her back against it.

He waited for her to move, trying to stay calm, trying to resist the urge to move her bodily aside, so he could leave, and close the door on this whole rotten episode. With a sigh, he said, "Shelley, please, I have to go…"

Her face registered all the emotions he knew her capable of – the pout which she thought was so sexy – and had been, once. Then, came the tears. And when all that failed, she lashed out.

The first four slaps he took, he owed her that much. But, as the onslaught continued, he grabbed her wrists, pressing her back against the door. "Stop it, Shelley. Do you want your neighbours to hear you?"

"I hate you!"

"Actually, I'm not too keen on myself right at this moment."

"I wish you were dead! Do you hear me?" she raged, her eyes blazing. "I wish you were dead!"

He released her. "The whole street can hear you. Do you really want them calling the police? Blabbing to your husband? Do you?"

Her face twisted with fury. Whatever charms he'd once seen in her were lost to him now. In a voice thick with malice, she hissed, "I *will* say you raped me. I will, damn you." Her lips parted ready to scream 'rape.'

She meant it. He saw it in her face. Horrified, he clamped his hand over her open mouth. "Stop it, Shelley! This is insane."

Viciously, she sank her teeth into his middle finger. The pain, for a second shocked him. He tried to pull away, but her teeth were clamped around his finger. He swung her round, slamming against her shoulder with his free hand. Her mouth opened as she reeled backwards, crashing onto the floor.

He hadn't meant to use such force. He felt suddenly sick. Fumbling for the bedroom door handle, he glanced back briefly, and then, pure gut reaction took over. She was back on her feet, and coming at him like someone possessed, nail scissors clutched in her hand.

His left arm shot up in defence, protecting his face. His forearm took the full force of the twin blades. Agonisingly, they stuck in his arm, sending two streams of blood trickling down his wrist. He brought his right hand back, and slapped her hard with the back of his hand across her jaw. She thudded to the floor, like a marionette with its strings cut.

For a second, he thought he'd killed her, and his stomach lurched. Then, thankfully, he saw the rise and fall of her breasts

He stood trembling, feeling ready to throw up, sickened by his own aggression towards a woman. It went against the grain, and everything he believed in. You didn't hit women. But, this was the cowardly bastard he'd turned into.

He hated leaving her semi-conscious, but staying would only prolong the aggravation. He pulled the scissors from the side of his wrist, and grabbed a handful of tissues to press over the puncture wounds, and around the bite on his finger. He stumbled out of her bedroom, down the stairs, and out into the fog.

He drove swiftly away from her house, putting as much distance as he could between them. Then, he pulled into the curb, and sat with the engine idling. He was shaking, the tissues were saturated, and blood was still trickling down his arm, soaking into his cuffs. Finding a handkerchief, he bound it around the wound, and drove. By the time he pulled into his driveway, the blood had started to congeal.

Julia's Mini wasn't there, and he guessed she'd put it in the garage. She sometimes did. It had more chance of starting when the weather was cold and damp, if it had been garaged overnight.

The house was in darkness. The heavy grey night shrouded the white walls and black timber framework. Only as he got close to the front door could he make out the rough twisted branches of the wisteria climbing the walls and erupting in brilliant blue flowers in summertime. Julia had planted it when they'd first bought the house, more than ten years ago, and it had first flowered the summer Lucy started school.

As he turned the key, he hoped Julia was asleep. It would be a struggle to explain the mess he was in. Besides, he was sick of lying and deceiving. If she was awake, he might blurt out the truth. That would be for the best. *Only, why hurt her? There was a faint chance she didn't know, and if that was the case, why put her through hell, to ease his conscience?*

No light shone from behind the patterned glass kitchen, lounge, or study doors leading off the hallway. He dropped his car keys on the little walnut telephone table, and listened to the silence of the house. The only sound was the ticking of the clock. It had been a wedding present from someone, he couldn't remember who. It was a relief not to find Julia up and waiting for him, although once, or twice, she'd fallen asleep on the sofa during her vigil. He hoped to God she hadn't done that tonight.

Keeping as silent as he could, he went through to the kitchen. There was a faint smell of cooking, but there wasn't a plate wrapped in tinfoil for him to re-heat, as there's been at the start of his late nights. She'd trusted him, really believed he was working late. It was these last couple of weeks she hadn't bothered to plate up any dinner. *Was she pissed off, because he was always late home, or had she guessed he was cheating?* He could only hope and pray he hadn't left it too late.

Peeling off his shirt, he rinsed as much of the blood out of it, and the handkerchief, as he could, all the while listening for Julia, praying she wouldn't wander sleepily into the kitchen, and find him like this. The house seemed silent, though, thankfully. He bundled the stained garments into the washing machine, but his jacket would have to go to the dry cleaners. He guessed he'd have to make up some excuse about injuring himself at work. More lies. He was so good at lying, these days.

He filled the kettle for a coffee, applied antiseptic to the puncture wounds on his wrist and finger, and covered them with two plasters. Catching sight of his reflection in the blackened window, he saw a clean cut, thirty-eight-year-old, a solid family man. The sort of guy who worked hard for his lovely wife and daughter, to give them the life they deserved. He didn't have a bad physique, lean, the hint of a six-pack. When Shelley had first seen him naked, she'd looked like the cat who'd got the cream. Like a fool, he'd revelled in the attention she'd lavished on him.

Sickened, he turned aside, knots tightening in his stomach like corkscrews. God, how he despised himself.

He made a coffee – strong and black, and drank it standing up. The first cup stemmed his trembling. The second calmed his breathing. The third would probably keep him awake half the night.

Finally, he plucked up the courage to peep into the lounge, and see if Julia had fallen asleep on the sofa. She hadn't, and so he crept upstairs, checking Lucy's bedroom first. Her bed was empty, which meant she was in their bed. She often slipped under the covers with them, if she'd had a bad dream. Neither of them got much sleep when that happened. So, that probably meant Julia was still awake. His heart sank.

Perhaps it would be better if he crashed out on the sofa, or on Lucy's bed, and not disturb them. *The coward's way out.* He knew that, and a nagging little voice in his head told him to face her. It was the least he could do.

There was a tightness in his throat, as he eased open their bedroom door. And then, his heart sank like a stone. For long, agonising minutes, he stood there, staring blankly at the undisturbed double bed, the silence of the house ringing in his ears. No wonder the house had felt so quiet. No wonder.

Gone. They've left you. The words jangled in his empty brain. *Gone. It was too late.* She knew.

There was an envelope propped up on his pillow. A pink envelope, with purple dragons on it. With a sinking heart, he opened it, flicked on the bedside lamp, and read the childish print on the rainbow coloured notepaper.

Dear Daddy, we have gone to Aunty Steph's.
I hope I'll see you soon.
Love and kisses from Lucy and Mister Brown.

His legs seemed to lose their strength, and he sank down onto the edge of the bed, eyes closed. It had been years since he'd cried. He'd almost forgotten what his tears tasted like.

Chapter 7

Julia had lost all track of time and reality. She drove mile after mile through swirling claustrophobic blackness. The world had become invisible, except for the two red tail lights of the car in front – and the face in her rear-view mirror.

It was a hideous face. Not because of the scar and the blood, but because of the look in his eyes. It was a face lacking compassion, vicious, and it was squashed up next to her sobbing daughter.

She didn't know whether he was holding a weapon to Lucy. His appearance was threatening enough. Because he was there, next to her little girl in the back seat of her Mini, Julia continued to follow the other car, as ordered.

"Don't be frightened, Lucy. It's going to be alright." In her heart, she prayed it would be. That they would stick to their word, take her car, and leave them to get home on foot. She clung to that hope. The alternative was too terrible to contemplate.

The child sobbed. "I want to go home…"

"Shut it!" the man snapped, causing Lucy to scream in fright, and then, sob all the more.

"Don't hurt her, please don't hurt her," Julia begged, her thoughts racing. *Could she stop the car, and pull Lucy out, before he caught hold of them? Before the man in the first car saw what was going on? Could they lose these two demons in the fog?*

"Just shut it," he repeated dully.

Julia continued driving, her right leg cramping, her knuckles white on the wheel. She spoke gently to her daughter. "Don't cry, Lucy, please don't cry. It'll only make things worse."

They had committed some crime, some atrocity to risk this.

"Where are we going?" Julia asked, afraid almost to speak, and terrified of what the answer might be. But, he made no reply, and glancing into her interior mirror, she saw his head had rolled back, and his eyes were shut.

Was he sleeping? She couldn't tell whether he was resting his eyes, or had fallen into unconsciousness. *Dare she veer away, and take her and Lucy to some place of safety? Would he notice? Could she lie to him, and make out she'd lost the other car's tail lights in the fog?*

She glanced again in the mirror, trying to gauge the depth of his drowsiness. But, then, the brake lights of the preceding car glowed brighter, as it drew to a halt. Julia slowed, wondering whether she dared to drive off now. The other man was out of the car ahead. If she was going to make a move, it had to be now.

Then, the man behind her stirred. "No tricks," he warned.

A moment later, the leather-coated man had yanked her car door open, turned off the ignition, and pocket the keys. "Not a peep out of you – or the kid. Understand?"

She watched him in her headlights, as he walked back to his car, and hauled four large holdalls from the boot of his vehicle. He attempted to transfer them to her Mini, and swore, as he saw her boot was already full with her suitcases. It only delayed him for a moment. He transferred her suitcases into his car, and clicked the boot lid shut. He brought the holdalls to the rear of her car, and loaded them in. The car dipped at the weight.

Joy riders, or burglars, that's what they were. They would dump her and Lucy here, and take her Mini. Yet, in her heart, she knew she was fooling herself. These weren't teenagers stealing cars for kicks – they were something far worse.

The leather-coated one strolled back to his car, as if he had all the time in the world. He reached into it, and seemed to be adjusting the handbrake and steering wheel. Then, walking to its rear, he leaned his back against the vehicle, moving it forward, all the while staring directly through her headlights into her eyes. Despite being unable to see his expression behind his mask, she had the feeling he was smirking. As if he was enjoying this.

Julia saw it then, a glimmer of water shimmering through the fog. She could smell the damp in the air. *It was a lake – no! It was the reservoir, that was where they were, the reservoir.* She gasped. He was pushing his car into the reservoir.

The red tail lights dipped to a precarious angle, and then, came the gurgling of water as it filled the vehicle, slowly dragging it down into a watery grave.

"Why is he doing that?" she whispered. "Why in God's name is he doing that?"

"Mummy, I want to go home."

"Soon," she breathed, feeling as if she were drowning herself. Drowning in a flood of terror. *What had these two done to make them push their car into a reservoir?*

Within moments, the car had totally disappeared from view, taking with it her suitcases with their clothes, sweaters, coats, Lucy's school uniform, everything. A sob caught in her throat.

Dusting off his hands, he walked back towards them, pulling his balaclava from his head, and smiling. Yes, she knew he'd be smiling. If the keys had still been in the ignition, then she would have run him down.

He leaned into the car, suffocating her with the smell and feel of his leather coat, but now, she could see his face, his flawless skin, his arrogant straight nose, the square hard jaw-line, his shaggy blond hair and dazzling smile – such perfect teeth. He was, she realised – quite perfect, and totally without conscience. Beautiful and evil, a terrible combination, and an icy chill ran through her veins.

His pale eyes switched to his accomplice, the smile was still in place. Pleasantly, he asked, "Feeling up to it, Nash?"

Up to what? She wanted to scream. *Drive? What else could he mean?* She didn't dare let her mind think of what he might mean.

The injured man groaned. "Can't, Vincent, not now. Not in this state."

"Later, then," he shrugged, turning his penetrating stare to her again… "Move over then, beautiful. I'll take the wheel now."

She tried to control the tremor in her voice. She knew both of their names. They'd let them slip. She'd seen their faces. *Where they stupid? Or was it because they had no intention of letting her and Lucy go?*

She needed to reason with them. "Look, I… I don't know what sort of trouble you two are in, but if you'll let my daughter and I get out, I swear we won't say a word."

His eyebrows arched. "What, leave two young ladies miles from anywhere? I wouldn't hear of it."

"But, you said if I followed you, you'd let us go. You'd take my car, and let us go!"

"I lied," he said, getting in, forcing her over into the passenger seat, and starting the car.

Julia's throat dried, she struggled to form the words. "Please, let us go. My little girl is only eight. You're terrifying her."

"Pretty little thing, isn't she?" he remarked, glancing back at Lucy. "So, you'll see to it later then, Nash?"

The other man mumbled a vague reply she couldn't decipher.

The bigger man looked back at her, a sympathetic expression on his face. "This fog is a bugger, isn't it?"

"Look, you have my word, we won't tell anyone anything," Julia begged, touching the cold leather sleeve, then recoiling, as she saw the sideways expression he cast her way.

"Women and their word," he said, uttering a harsh laugh. "The two don't equate in my book." Then, putting the car into gear, he drove.

Julia sat, half turned in her seat, reaching across, and clutching Lucy's cold hand, stroking it, trying to calm her. The bloodied individual had slumped again, lolling whichever way the car veered, sometimes leaning all over Lucy, sometimes bumping against the side window. Lucy's eyes were awash with tears, and at that moment, Julia hated Ian, almost as much as she hated these two. If it hadn't been for him, Lucy would still be tucked up safely in bed, instead of being held captive by these two monsters.

They drove a further twenty minutes or so, before he turned off to the left. Although there was little to see beyond the headlights, it seemed to Julia this was a narrow lane with sharp twists and hairpin bends. Tall hedgerows flanked both sides of her car, sometimes catching the metal with overgrown twigs. He took another turn, slowing, and she heard the sound of gravel under the wheels.

They came to a halt beneath the gloomy shadow of a derelict house. It towered over them, huge, three stories high, at least. The one called Vincent gave her a smile, as he got out. If it was meant to reassure her they would be okay, it had the opposite effect. It chilled her to the bone. Her throat tightened. It was almost impossible to comprehend how someone, who spoke so elegantly and had such a handsome face, could terrorise a woman and child in this way.

In her heart, she sensed this one, Vincent, was the worst of the two. At least she hoped the pathetic, semi-conscious younger man, Nash, wasn't any more despicable, or brutal.

"Out you get, beautiful, but mind you don't do anything silly, because my friend, Nash here, has your little girl. Hold her hand tightly now, Nash."

Julia got out quickly, reaching into the back to swiftly unbuckle Lucy. She swept the child, and her handbag up into her arms. "Don't you touch her!"

As Lucy's arms clamped around her neck, Julia noticed the pool of blood on the floor of her car. It couldn't all have come from Nash's head injury. It seemed to be seeping down from his arm.

Shivering with cold and fear, she stared up at the house. It oozed desolation. It was old and rotting, she could smell the decay from here. Windows were boarded up, and there was a keep out sign nailed to the front door, saying the house was dangerous and condemned. She clung however to a tiny thread of hope. Her phone was in her bag. She recalled throwing it in earlier. At the first opportunity, she'd call for help, and it had that tracking device, which she didn't understand, but which she knew she had, because she'd suggested once to Ian his ought to be switched on like hers. He'd laughed her suggestion away. She knew why – now she knew why. She looped the shoulder strap round her neck, and slid the bag under her coat.

"Home! Be it ever so humble," said Vincent, with a sweep of his arm. "After you."

She had no choice but to walk, and she carried Lucy along a pathway around the side of the house towards the rear. The broken concrete slabs were smothered in dead wet leaves, making it slippery. It began to rain.

The wood of the back door was rotten, and Vincent did nothing more than turn the handle, and give the door a sharp shove to open it. He held it for Julia, like the perfect gentleman, expecting her to step into the black stinking void within. She held back, refusing to go in, frantically looking round for some means of escape. The fog and darkness made it impossible to see more than a few yards ahead.

"Nash, help the lady carry the little girl inside. We don't want them falling over and hurting themselves, do we now?"

"You're not touching her!" Julia cried, clutching Lucy fiercely. *Oh God, why hadn't she left Lucy safely in her bed?* If only she could turn back the clock. "Lucy, I'm sorry, I'm so sorry."

A sharp jab in her kidney made her cry out.

"Oh! Did I hurt you?" Vincent asked apologetically. "Only, do go in, it's rather chilly out here."

Vincent – what a name, what a gentle, civilised name to be attached to such a despicable individual.

"Get in, will you," the other one mumbled, stumbling past her. "I need bandaging... I'm still bleeding, Vince... and my head... Christ, everything kills."

Julia shuddered, and Lucy buried her face into her neck, as she took her daughter inside. The house stank of rot and mildew, and something scampered underfoot. "Where are we?"

"Home sweet home. Not exactly the Ritz, but it will suffice, for the time being," said Vincent, putting a match to a camping paraffin lamp. His face and the room flickered into view.

"You live here?" Julia murmured.

No one could live here, it was decaying and filthy. There were a few bits of furniture – a huge old Welsh dresser against the wall, a table, a couple of chairs, some boxes, but great chunks of plaster were missing from the walls. There were holes in the ceiling. The floorboards felt damp and pliable underfoot. Yet, there was evidence the place was being lived in. There was a carton of milk and a bottle of water on the sink draining board, a loaf of bread wrapped in cellophane, a box of eggs, a jar of coffee. But, the place reeked of rot and death – a sickening smell.

In the shifting pale light, Julia beheld the injured man properly for the first time. He was in a dreadful mess. His pallor behind the streaks of blood, was grey. He had clearly lost a lot of blood from his injuries. He slumped down onto a wooden chair, and lowered his head onto the table.

Despite everything, Julia turned on Vincent. "This man needs proper medical attention. He's badly hurt."

Vincent's mouth curled into that ready smile, which he no doubt thought was irresistible. "Ah! Isn't that touching, Nash. The little lady is worried about you."

Lucy suddenly wailed loudly. "I want my daddy!"

"I know, my darling, I know," Julia murmured, cradling her, rocking her in her arms. "We'll see him again soon, I promise."

Nash stumbled to the sink, and turned on the tap. A trickle of brown water spewed out. He put his wrist under the flow.

"Are you trying to make yourself worse?" Julia exclaimed. "That water is filthy. Those injuries need proper attention, or you're going to get infected." Even as she spoke, she realised the insaneness of it. She wished he would die of infection right this minute – the both of them.

With his arms in the filthy sink, Nash turned his head to stare at her with dull, half dead eyes. "Got any better ideas?"

Shocked by the state of him, Julia turned back to Vincent. There was a thought at the back of her mind if she could get these two working against each other, it might take the attention from her and Lucy, long enough for them to run. "This man is dying. He needs a doctor now!"

Vincent uttered a brittle laugh. "He's okay, aren't you, Nash? He's a bit of a baby when it comes to blood – well, his own blood, anyhow. Isn't that right, my old mate?"

Nash propped himself against the sink. "Dunno. Feel faint, Vince."

Julia glared at the bigger man. "If you're any sort of friend, you've got to get him to a doctor, or a hospital. He's lost a lot of blood."

Vincent reacted swiftly. The sneering smile vanished, and he thrust his face within inches of hers. Lucy cried out in fright, and buried herself even deeper into her mother's neck. Julia tried not to flinch, even though she could feel his breath on her skin, smell the leather of his coat, and could see her own wide-eyed face mirrored back in his eyes. Somehow, she found the courage to glare right back at him, into those soulless pale eyes, determined not to show how terrified she was of him.

"You fix him up, then," he said, dangerously softly. "Women are supposed to be good at that sort of thing. You fix him up. You stop him from dying."

She held her ground, held his stare. Her voice was little more than a whisper as she replied, "Why the hell should I?"

Two small patches of pink appeared in his cheeks, as she continued to stare back at him. His expression distorted. What anyone would have described as a classically handsome face disappeared behind a sneer twisting his features into something far worse than his companion's.

Julia was positive it was only because she was holding Lucy she didn't buckle in fear. The intensity of his eyes seemed to draw all strength from her body. She clung tighter to her daughter, keeping the child's eyes averted from him. Her heart was pounding, knowing it was a mistake to stand up to him. He expected submissiveness. She prayed it wasn't a grave mistake, and braced herself for the blow, the punch; the snapping of her neck she felt was coming at any second.

Then, Nash whimpered, "Someone's gotta help me."

It was as if a bubble had burst. The sneer turned back to a smile, and Vincent eased back. Holding out an outstretched arm towards his accomplice, he said, "Because he has asked you so nicely – good enough for m'lady?"

It felt like her heart had lodged itself in her throat. Somehow, she stemmed the quaver in her voice. Somehow, she conjured up a brusqueness that she didn't know she possessed. "I'll need the lamp over here, and some sort of antiseptic and bandages. I hope you've got power to boil this water."

Without a word, he put a match to a paraffin camping stove, filled a kettle with water from the bottle, and placed it on the ring. His tone, when he spoke, was sickeningly condescending. "All mod cons here, you know. And, maybe, you'd like a coffee while you're working on him?"

Julia made no reply, but was glad of the flame that provided a little warmth, as it popped into life. "Stand here, Lucy," she murmured, trying to set Lucy down beside her, but the child clung fiercely to her, arms and legs tight around her body. "Please, Lucy, here, right next to me."

Reluctantly, the child allowed herself to be set down. Julia wrapped the blanket tightly around the child, tucking her teddy bear inside with her. "There! You hold Mister Brown nice and tightly, okay?"

She nodded, her eyes swimming with tears and fear.

"Don't be frightened, sweetheart. We'll be home soon." To Vincent, she said, "I need some clean cloth, something to bathe his wounds with, and bandages."

Vincent's gaze lingered over her. "Bossy little madam, aren't you?"

She shuddered under his scrutiny, but somehow tilted her chin determinedly. "Do you want your friend to bleed to death?"

"Vince, help us, mate," Nash groaned. "Use one of me shirts. It don't matter about ripping it up. There's one in me bag upstairs."

Julia saw the irritation pass over Vincent's face. He didn't take kindly to being told what to do. It was obvious who was in change in this set up. He said nothing to the injured man, but glanced towards the back door, which he'd bolted after them. Her eyes followed his, heartened to know there's been no key turned, and the bolt was within reach. At the very first opportunity, she and Lucy would be out of here.

Vincent saw her looking, and cocked one eyebrow. "Now then, can I trust you not to do a runner while I'm getting the bandages for our friend here?" He rubbed his chin. "Nope! I don't believe I can."

Before Julia could make any false promises, he grabbed Lucy and dragged her to him, holding her around her throat. The child squealed in terror.

Julia went for him. "Leave her alone!"

But, he swung her around, keeping her at a distance, avoiding Julia's nails as she clawed at his face, and would have gauged out his eyes, given half a chance.

Backing off, still holding Lucy in a stranglehold, he held out his other hand. "Insurance, that's all. She can help me carry the stuff down."

His voice was soothing. It terrified her.

"You'll help your Uncle Vincent, won't you, Lucy?" he asked, backing away from Julia, loosening his grip a fraction.

"You're not my uncle," Lucy shrieked, kicking backwards at his ankles.

"If I say I am, then I am," Vincent uttered, his lips drawn back across perfect white teeth. "Now, are you coming upstairs nicely to help your Uncle Vincent, or am I going to have to get cross?"

For a second, no one spoke, no one moved. Julia was ready to lunge at him, if he gave any indication he was going to hurt Lucy. Finally, wide-eyed, Lucy murmured, "All right."

Julia's heart lurched. Even an eight-year-old could recognise the danger facing them.

He smiled, released his stranglehold on her, and took her hand. "What a sensible little girl you have here. What is your name, by the way?"

Julia didn't want to tell him, but somewhere at the back of her mind, she was recalling TV documentaries, and how studies show captives had more chance of a safe release, if they got to know their jailers, and they got to know their prisoners. Reluctantly, she said, "Julia. And my husband will have the police out looking for us by now. Please, release us. I promise we won't say anything."

A deliberate frown creased his forehead. His mouth twisted, as if puzzled by something. "Now I'm no Sherlock Holmes, but I couldn't help but notice there were suitcases in your boot, and your daughter is in her nightdress. Correct me if I'm wrong, but I'd say you left in a bit of a hurry. I'd say, your husband will think you've left him. I don't think he'll be expecting you home for a long time."

She couldn't answer, and she knew one thing for sure. He wasn't stupid.

Lucy's blanket and the teddy she'd been clutching fell to the floor, as he led her away. He spoke over one shoulder, "We won't be long."

"Don't you hurt her!" Julia screamed after him. "You harm one hair on her head, and I swear I'll not lift a finger to help your friend. I'll see him bleed to death first."

The shrug of his shoulders spoke of how little he cared, and how futile her threat was.

Desperation gripped her. She grabbed the injured man's arm, forcing him to look at her. His gaze was blank, lost in a world of his own, hardly aware of what was going on. "Tell him!" she screamed at Nash, shaking him. "You tell him now!"

From beneath half shuttered eyes, Nash mumbled, "Hurry up, Vince mate. If someone don't stop me bleeding in a minute, I'm done for."

Smiling to himself, Vincent led Lucy out of the room.

Chapter 8

Shelley de Main stared at her reflection in the bathroom mirror. Her eyes were still puffy from the bout of hysterical crying she'd had after coming around, and finding Ian had gone. But, all the crying in the world wasn't going to bring him back. Not that she'd have him back now, after the way he had treated her.

"Bastard!" she spat, soaking another wad of cotton wool in witch-hazel, and dabbing it over the purple swelling at the side of her mouth where he'd hit her.

She hadn't expected him to lash out. The stupid man couldn't really have thought she was going to stick him with the scissors; it was a gesture. Catching him with the blades was an accident, and she would be certain to tell him that, if they ever spoke again. However, she would never forgive him for smacking her in the face.

She wished now she had got him with the scissors properly. In the neck—that would have served him right. No more than he deserved – leading her on, using her. He made her sick. *Where had his damn conscience been for the last four months?* Nowhere, because it suited him to forget he had a wife and kid. Then, once he'd had his fun, he wanted out. *Well, Mister 'Happily Married' Ian Logan – you are in for a shock.*

She dabbed her chin with a towel, filled a glass with water, and took it back to bed, dosing herself with some pain killers. Roger's shift didn't finish for another hour, but she doubted the purple swelling would have gone by then. Most likely, the bruise would be worse. *How the hell was she going to explain it away?* She was going to have to come up with something pretty good. Roger wasn't stupid. Boring, yes, but not stupid.

"Damn you, Ian Logan," she murmured, as she slid back between the cool, silky sheets. "You were a waste of time anyway."

When they first started seeing each other, the sex had been incredible, but these last few weeks had been difficult. Thinking back, she realised it was obvious he'd been cooling towards her. "Fool!" she murmured to herself. She ought to have dumped him, instead of hanging on. "Bloody fool!"

She stared up at the ceiling, her eyes filling with tears again, hurting almost as much as her bruised face. "Fuck you, Ian Logan. Fuck you, and your fucking stupid conscience."

The sound of the key turning in the lock, an hour and a half later, made her stomach muscles tighten. Roger was home. She swung her legs out of bed, pulled a dressing gown on, and checked her appearance in the mirror. She had two choices. If the bruising had faded, she'd say nothing, and hope none of the neighbours had heard her shouting earlier. If the bruising was noticeable, she'd have to come up with something convincing.

She couldn't really stick to her threat, and tell Roger she'd been raped. He'd drag the police in; he was bound to. And an examination would soon show she hadn't been touched. *What a shame. It would have been so nice to drag Mister Clean Ian Logan's name through the mud.*

She was sitting on the edge of her bed, wringing at a handkerchief anxiously, when, ten minutes later, the bedroom door opened silently, so as not to wake her. She was always asleep when he came home, or at least pretending to be.

"Hello, still awake, love? What's the matter?"

She turned to him, tears sparkling convincingly in her mascara-smeared eyes.

"Shelley? What's up, love?"

He sat beside her on the bed, still smelling of the factory. As a hands-on factory owner, he threw himself into the job. Most women would be proud of such a husband, who had made a success of his business, provided a beautiful home, cars, clothes, holidays. But, inside, she was screaming to tell him not to sit on the bed in his work clothes. However, this wasn't the time.

She turned on the tears, with a mournful expression on her face. "Thank goodness you're home. Oh, Roger, it was dreadful."

His frown creased right up past his receding hairline. "Shelley… what's happened? What was dreadful?"

Such a pity she couldn't put the blame on Ian, but she didn't dare risking Roger even getting an inkling of what had been going on behind his back. She had too much to lose. She would find some other opportunity to get her revenge, that was for sure.

"I've been mugged!" Shelley sobbed, pleased with the way she could make herself tremble. "Coming back from the cinema. Some awful teenager, in one of those hoody things, snatched my bag, and when I tried to stop him, he punched me in the face, and I fell down. Oh Roger, it hurts so much."

"You poor lamb," he said, wrapping her in his arms, cradling her, stroking her hair, cajoling her with words of sympathy. She did her best not to cringe. And then, he set her aside. "He won't get away with it. I'm calling the police."

"No!" she cried sharply. "I… I don't want to talk about it. It was too awful. I want to forget it. There was only a few pounds in my purse anyway—no cards or anything important."

"That's not the point. The man hit you," Roger said, dark angry patches of red mottling his neck. "No, Shelley, he can't get away scot free. I'm calling the police."

She couldn't stop him, and as he marched out of the bedroom, Shelley felt herself seething with anger and frustration, and hatred for Ian Logan. It was one thing to lie to her husband, but lying to the police would be way more difficult. They would want to know exactly where it happened, what time, a description of her bag and purse, and a description of the attacker. *Oh Lord! Why hadn't she said she'd hit herself on a cupboard door?* God, she was so stupid at times. She didn't even know what films were showing. And there were CCTV cameras everywhere, and she wouldn't be on any of them.

Downstairs, she could hear Roger on the phone. She moved swiftly, opening the internet on her mobile, and finding the local cinema information. She only hoped there would be something she'd seen before, so she knew the plot, if asked. With luck, she could still talk her way out of this mess bloody Ian Logan had got her into.

But, he wasn't going to get away with this. She would make him pay, if it took her to the end of her days.

Chapter 9

Julia counted the seconds, straining her ears for her daughter's cries. Their footsteps upstairs echoed through the house. She prayed under her breath, desperately wanting to warn Lucy the floorboards might be rotten, and she might fall through. She prayed harder *he* would fall through the ceiling, and break his neck.

She couldn't bear it any longer, and went to go after them. Suddenly, a bloody arm came violently around her throat, catapulting her backwards.

"He ain't gonna touch her."

"Am I supposed to believe that?" she cried, almost hysterical with fear for her daughter.

"You ain't got no choice. You're staying put." Reinforcing his words, he dragged a metal bar from his pocket, and pushed it under her chin.

Julia was sure there were blood stains on it, as she stared into his half-closed eyes. His horrible skin was pock-marked and grey, with grime caked into the holes where he must have been stitched at one time. His skin was rumpled, and looked as if it had been tugged back into place. No wonder he hated the world.

The lump of metal under her chin made it almost impossible to speak, but she had to try. "If you use that on me, I won't be able to bandage your wounds."

He stared at her for only a few more moments, and then, as if it was all too exhausting, he laid the weapon on the table, and sank back down onto the chair.

Julia's eyes flitted from him to the lump of metal. *Could she grab it? Had she the strength to hit him so hard, it would put him totally out of action? But, then what?* She doubted she could overpower the bigger man – and he had Lucy.

So, she waited, listening to her heart thudding, while floorboards creaked overhead, and ice ran through her veins.

After what seemed like an eternity, Lucy came running through the door at the far side of the room. "Mummy…"

"Oh my God, you're alright!" she gasped, racing past Nash to gather Lucy up in her arms. "Thank God, thank God."

"Give your mother the shirt to rip up, Lucy," Vincent instructed, sauntering past them, smirking.

"It's horrible upstairs, Mummy," Lucy whispered. "It's smelly and dark, and the stairs wobble when you go up them."

"Did he touch you?" Julia whispered back. "Did he hurt you, love?"

The child shook her head.

Breathing a silent prayer, she kissed Lucy, and gently set her aside. With trembling hands, she tried ripping the shirt into strips. It was impossible. "I can't do this."

A knife appeared under her nose. The blade was as long as her forearm, and Vincent's smooth fingers were gripped around the bone handle. "Allow me to assist."

For a second, Julia thought she would throw up. He'd delighted in revealing the weapon. It was clearly a threat. He was enjoying every minute of this. Julia wondered if he had a mother or a sister, or a girlfriend. She should ask him. Make him think how he'd feel if someone were terrorising them.

But, no words formed, and she stood, holding onto Lucy, staring at the slick way he sliced the shirt into strips.

She knew it was deliberate how, every now and then, he shifted his eyes from the knife to her and Lucy, as if at any second he would use that blade to slit all their throats. She wanted to be sick.

The nauseous feeling didn't pass, even when he'd finished the job, and slid the knife back inside his trench coat.

He stepped aside, extending an arm, as if to invite her to now assess his companion's injuries. She moved Lucy to the other side of her, as far away from this pair as she could.

"Push your jacket sleeve up, or take it off," she told Nash.

"I'll bloody freeze to death, if I take it off," he complained, easing the hard blood soaked denim back up his arm to reveal the wound.

Julia did her best not to gag. The wound was horrific. A piece of flesh, as big as her fist, had been torn out of his inner wrist, and hung there by a sliver of skin. It oozed thick, wine-coloured blood.

"This needs stitching," she told them, looking from one to the other. "And you need a transfusion. If it wasn't for the tourniquet, you'd be dead already."

Vincent looked pleased with himself. "Hey! I saved your life. Remember that, matey."

Julia felt utterly sickened, as Nash cast his accomplice a grateful nod. Angrily, she added, "He might still die without a transfusion, and proper treatment."

"Just bandage him up tight. That'll do the trick."

Julia glared at the leather-clad figure. "Don't you care if he dies?"

The injured man turned his head slowly to look at him, a questioning look in his eye. Julia saw, with surprise, the flinching of muscles in Vincent's cheek, and the fidgeting of his body in discomfort, as his wretched accomplice continued to stare at him, awaiting his verdict. *Did he care whether Nash lived or died?* The question intrigued her, too.

Vincent's arrogance gave way to a sickly concern "Of course I care, but Nash isn't about to snuff it. Strong as an ox, aren't you, mate?"

The honeyed tones may have fooled Nash, but they didn't fool her. She had thought Vincent was the leader, when actually, he was in awe of Nash—an awe bordering on fear. She stored this knowledge away, as if it was ammunition. She was only too aware she was no match for them, physically. But, she had her wits – and her determination to get her and Lucy away safely. She prayed it would be enough.

"Just bandage me up tight, like Vince says," Nash mumbled, turning his head aside.

Gritting her teeth, Julia began to patch him together. Vincent averted his eyes, too, clearly sickened. As she worked, her anger burned. So, Vincent was offended by the hideousness of his accomplice's condition, yet took great pains not to let him know, out of a deep-seated trepidation. *But, if someone as cold-hearted as Vincent was afraid of his injured partner, how dangerous was this wretched individual?*

She inspected the misshapen face, splintered with fragments of broken windscreen, caked with dried blood, and wondered how he had gotten so badly disfigured. The old scar running down his face resembled a knife wound. But, the ragged gash to his forearm looked like a dog bite. *Had he broken into someone's house, and disturbed the householder, or their dog?* She instantly remembered hearing a dog barking, when she was watching for Ian. It had sounded like Benjamin's collie.

Was that it? Had they broken into Benjamin Stanton's house? Her throat tightened in horror. *Was Benjamin alright? Had they hurt him? Had they killed him? And, if they'd killed once, what was to stop them killing again?*

Her skin prickled with terror, as if a million needles were being jabbed into her. *Was she supposed to stop this maniac from bleeding to death, so they could murder her and Lucy?*

She hadn't stopped shaking since the collision, but now the trembling became worse, and she began shaking so badly, the strips of cloth kept slipping from her fumbling fingers. Nash dragged a hard-backed chair towards him with his foot, and nodded for her to sit down on it next to him. Lucy stood close, cocooned in her blanket again, her face tiny and ghost-like.

Julia worked silently on Nash's injuries, painstakingly removing the splinters of glass from his flesh, cringing and ridiculously apologising for the pain she was inflicting. She cleansed each tiny cut with boiled water. There was no antiseptic. Infection would probably set in, but there was nothing she could do about that.

Vincent made coffee, placing a cup beside her, as if they were enjoying a pleasant interlude. Reluctantly, Julia sipped it. The mug was chipped and grimy, but the strong liquid revived her brain, helped her to think ahead, beyond this nightmare, to how she and Lucy were going to get away. They *would* get free. No matter what these two were intending, she would get her daughter away from here, somehow.

The sound of music startled her. Vincent was playing something through his mobile, and had straddled one of the other chairs, his chin resting on his folded arms along the back, like he hadn't a care in the world.

Julia didn't know the name of the band playing, but it was a familiar song, one Lucy sang along to, sometimes. She forced back her tears.

With Nash's arm bandaged as tightly as she could, and the patch of red that had immediately soaked through the bandages getting no worse, she put his arm in a sling. She fastened the knot four or five times behind his head, securing his arm tightly to his chest.

"Is that comfortable?" she asked, feeling as if she were betraying herself and Lucy by showing concern.

"What's with the sling? It ain't broken."

"The less you use it, the less chance you'll have of bleeding to death," she reminded him, not about to divulge her primary reason. Immobilising his arm had lessened the odds against her and Lucy, if only by a fraction.

Concentrating next on picking out the last fragments of glass from his forehead, she felt the crawling sensation of his other hand slipping under her coat, pawing her thigh.

She leapt back, sending her chair skittering across the floor. "Keep your hands off me!"

Lucy screamed, and clung to her.

The good side of Nash's mouth curved into what could have been a grin.

Vincent watched, one eyebrow arched. "You'd rather he played with your pretty little daughter?"

"Touch her, and I'll kill you."

They both laughed.

"Mummy…" Lucy murmured, hiding behind her.

"I'm too knackered anyhow," Nash grumbled, slurring his words.

The music faded on Vincent's mobile, and someone spoke. He'd tuned into the local radio, Julia recognised the late-night DJ. It was the three am news bulletin.

He turned up the volume. "Shut it. I want to hear if there's anything yet."

They all listened as the latest political squabbles were reported, along with an earthquake in a town Julia had never heard of, and an accident on the M6, with police blaming reckless drivers going too fast in the fog. Julia eased Lucy a little further towards the door, wondering if now was the time to make a run for it. Yet, she knew one move would have Vincent leaping at them. She would wait, bide her time, wait for the right moment.

There was a contented smirk on Vincent's face, as the weather report came on. He clicked his mobile off. "Nothing yet, mate."

"Good."

Julia leaned against a damp wall, cradling Lucy to her. Whatever these two demons had done, it was bad enough to make the news. Her heart cried silently out. *Ian, why did you do this to us?*

She closed her eyes. It was no use blaming him. It was her fault. She ought to have faced him with their problems, instead of running away.

She put her lips close to her daughter's ear. "Lucy," she whispered. "Did you tell Daddy in your letter where we were going?"

The child nodded. "Yes. Aunty Steph's."

"Good girl. When he rings her, and finds out we haven't arrived, he'll tell the police. They'll come looking for us…"

"It's rude to whisper," Vincent interrupted, standing up, kicking his chair aside. The clatter of wood made them jump.

As he sauntered closer to them, Julia felt her skin crawl with terror. She backed away, keeping Lucy tucked behind her. Ian *had* to ring Steph. *Please God*, she implored under her breath, *let him ring Steph before it was too late.*

He towered over them, broad-shouldered and powerful. Icy blue eyes sweeping over her slowly, from head to toe. His hands slid down the front of his coat, and she saw the silver buttons and the leather were streaked with blood. *Nash's blood – or someone else's? Benjamin's, maybe?*

She inched away, recoiling inwardly, keeping Lucy locked behind her, shielding her from this maniac. Her terror rose, as he began unbuttoning his long leather coat. The knife was tucked inside a deep pocket. She couldn't see it, but knew it was there. He stood a few inches from her, coat open revealing a lean athletic torso. He was all in black – a black sweater, black tight fitting jeans. He knew he looked good. No doubt he thought he was irresistible.

"Get away from us," she said, through gritted teeth.

His eyebrows arched innocently. "I was only going to ask if you'd care for more coffee?"

"Just let us go. My husband will have alerted the police by now. Whatever you've done, you don't want us on your conscience, too."

He stood with his hands on his hips, the heavy leather coat pushed back. "Oh, but we like the company. Don't we, Nash?"

Nash said nothing. He had his head down on the kitchen table, eyes shut.

Vincent inched closer, his index finger trailing from her throat down to her breasts. He fingered the zip of her coat. "And such attractive company."

She didn't flinch. If he expected her to look away, or avoid eye contact, he was in for a disappointment. Whatever harm he intended, he would have her face on his conscience forever. In a whisper, she breathed, "You have my word we won't tell a soul. Please, let us go."

For several drawn-out seconds, he said nothing. Then, with a glance at his accomplice, he said, "That's something my friend and I will have to consider, won't we, Nash?"

The other man made no reply. He looked asleep – or unconscious.

"Tomorrow, I think, when he's up to it. As for tonight, I think it's time we got a little shut-eye." He smiled. "Not here, though. I should hate you to slip out, and get lost. Upstairs, I think." He extended his arm towards the far doorway. "There's no need for me to use undue force, is there? You look like an intelligent woman. So, would you like to take yourself and your daughter upstairs to bed?

Left with no alternative, Julia lifted Lucy into her arms.

"Would you like me to carry her?"

Julia cast him a contemptuous glare, and walked ahead, Lucy's arms and legs wrapped fiercely around her.

The hallway leading to the staircase was draughty, bleak, and bitterly cold. The front door was bolted top and bottom, possibly nailed up. She couldn't tell. The precarious staircase shook and shuddered as they climbed, the bannister rotting and broken. Vincent followed at her heels, with the paraffin lamp casting horrendous shadows along the wall.

There was a rickety balcony on the first landing, and then, another flight of stairs to climb, worse than the first. Julia hesitated, only to be jabbed sharply in the back, urging her onwards. Terrified, she climbed, expecting the stairs to disintegrate underfoot at any second.

Somehow, they reached the top landing, without the entire staircase collapsing like a pack of cards. She doubted they would withstand much more use, though. This place was a death trap.

"There's a nice little room at the far end," Vincent said, like some estate agent showing prospective buyers around a desirable property.

The floorboards bowed beneath her feet, as she walked along the passageway. She could feel the rotten wood bending and groaning with every step. She moved slower, inching her way, as if she were walking on eggshells, their shadows on the wall looking nightmarish.

"You actually live here?" Julia asked, finding him too close, almost on top of her.

"Let's say, it's a sort of un-rented apartment while we're between homes. We'll be moving on to pastures newer and greener tomorrow."

"And what about us? I imagine we've complicated your plans."

Vincent moved past her, and opened a door. Again, his hand pressed into the small of her back, forcing her inside.

It was like walking into a tomb. If there was a window, it had been boarded up, although there was a draught blowing in from somewhere. The cold and damp seeped through to her bones, while the smell of mildew from dank walls invaded her senses.

"My partner sorts out the complications," he said, blowing her a kiss. "Sleep well, beautiful."

He closed the door with a bang, cutting off the meagre light source. Total impenetrable blackness closed around them, along with a suffocating sensation of claustrophobia. Lucy began to sob.

"Leave us the lamp," Julia shouted. He didn't answer, but she could hear him moving about outside in the passageway, as if looking for something. And then, he was back outside their door. She felt the handle move a few times, and then, came the groaning of the stairs beneath his weight as he went back down. She prayed with all her heart the stairs would collapse under him that very minute.

"I want to go home," Lucy sobbed. "I want my daddy!"

"I know, I know, sweetheart. We'll be out of here soon," she said, trying to sound confident. Once they were asleep, they'd be able to slip out, and get away. Cautiously, she tried to open the door, to peep out, but it opened a fraction and no more. She yanked at it furiously, not caring about the noise she was making. But, he'd secured it somehow.

"Pull it harder, Mummy!"

"It won't budge. He's tied it up." Her thoughts were racing. *Had she a pair of nail scissors in her bag?* She could ease them through the gap, try and cut through the rope, or whatever was holding them. But, as quick as the thought struck her, the answer came back as quickly. Her nail scissors were in her shower bag, in her suitcase, at the bottom of the reservoir.

"It's okay, sweetheart," she breathed, setting Lucy down, and dragging her bag out from under her coat. "I've got my mobile." She fumbled through it finding her make up bag, her purse, her hairbrush – but no phone. She searched again, getting Lucy to hold onto every item, as she pulled one thing after another out. Frantically now, she checked and double-checked the zipped compartments. Turning the whole thing inside out, pulling and pressing the lining, shaking the bag in desperation.

A silent shriek was building up from the pit of her stomach, threatening her sanity. Only the sight of Lucy's hopeful face peering up into hers stopped her from giving way to panic.

She buried her face into the child's hair, smelling the strawberry-scented shampoo she had used on her a few hours ago, and her heart broke.

Chapter 10

Ian's eyes felt puffed and heavy when he awoke. A check of his alarm clock showed it wasn't yet six, but he had done all the sleeping he could do. The bed was empty without Julia. The house was empty without her and Lucy.

Pushing back the covers, he slid his legs out and sat on the edge, head in hands. The rainbow-coloured note had fallen to the floor during the night. He picked it up again, and re-read it.

His own stupidity crippled him. He'd let the two people he loved most in the world slip out of his life. *And for what?* A fling with an older woman, not even a serious relationship, just sex. She'd shocked him, though, the way she'd come at him with those scissors. Talk about a woman scorned.

He dragged himself along to the bathroom, brushed his teeth, and peeled the plasters off his wrist and finger. Both wounds were still inflamed. He applied more antiseptic and plasters, and went downstairs.

He hesitated by the telephone in the hall. No point in ringing Stephanie this time of morning; they wouldn't be up. Probably when Julia got to her sister's last night, they would have put Lucy to bed, and sat discussing his failings long into the night. No, they wouldn't be up yet. He would ring later.

He made himself a cup of strong black coffee, and took it through to the lounge, working out what he'd say to Julia. He'd have to come clean, tell her the truth. There was no point in lying now. He owed her the truth, at the very least – and a massive apology, if she would accept it.

The whine of the electric milk float and jingle of milk bottles roused him from his thoughts, and he peered through the curtains. The fog had lifted, giving way to a dull grey morning. He watched the milkman leaving the milk on his own doorstep, then disappear down Benjamin Stanton's driveway. People in this street were old school – still having their milk delivered. If Julia wasn't back by tomorrow, he would have to nip round, and tell Benjamin she wouldn't be doing his shopping this week, and he'd have to make other arrangements. He ought to offer to do it, seeing as it was his fault Julia wasn't about. Yes, he'd probably do that. He'd certainly think about it, anyway.

Wandering back into the kitchen, he cooked himself a couple of rashers of bacon, threw in an egg, and watched them sizzle. He ate automatically, tasting nothing.

He couldn't go into work, not today. He rang in, and left a voice message on the boss's phone. He didn't want to talk to him either, even though Tony Wyndham was as much a friend as a boss. He couldn't face anyone, at the moment. Perhaps he should drive over to Stephanie's, see Julia for himself. See if she would talk to him.

No, it was too soon. Give her time. It was up to her whether she wanted him back. And she would need time to make up her mind. Better if he rang later.

At nine am, he emptied the pockets of his jacket, and took a walk down to the dry cleaners, needing the cold air to clear his mind, and get his thoughts together. By the time he got home, Julia should be back at her sister's, after taking Lucy to school. Steph worked full time, so Julia would probably be in the house on her own, hoping he might phone.

There was broken glass in the road near his house. He guessed there must have been a bump last night. Not surprising, with all the fog about. He kicked it into the gutter. The last thing he needed was a puncture, on top of everything else.

Back home, he picked up the phone, and dialled Steph's number. Eventually it clicked through to the answer phone, and he hung up. His insides felt like they'd tied themselves into a knot. *Was Julia listening to the ringing, knowing it was him, and deliberately not answering?* He picked up the receiver again, this time began dialling Julia's mobile number. He got through to the fifth digit, and then stopped. *What the hell was he going to say?*

For long agonising minutes he stared at the phone, and then, furious with himself, and his own stupidity, he slammed it down again, strode over to the cabinet, and poured himself a large whisky. About to turn away, instead, he picked up the bottle, and sank down into an armchair, bottle and glass in hand.

He didn't have any excuses to give Julia for his behaviour, but perhaps the bottle of scotch would supply one.

Chapter 11

Vincent awoke feeling good. The haul from the old bloke's place was going to set him up for a long time. It was top quality antique silver and gold, worth a bomb. Pity he'd have to halve the take with that little runt.

Nash deserved fuck all, seeing as he hadn't lifted a finger throughout the whole episode, and then, he'd turned into a liability, a weight around his neck. *He'd* had to do the dirty work, and killing really wasn't his style. Nash was going to have to earn his share by getting rid of the woman and the kid. That was something he couldn't do, not in cold blood, only if he had to, in the heat of the moment. Once that was done, they could drive her car down to London, unload the stuff, and he and Nash could split. He would never have to look at that ugly mug again.

It was going to be a busy morning.

He yawned, his hands going down the inside of his pants. First, though, he would give the cow one last thrill.

He crawled off the mattress, stood up and stretched. His jeans lay neatly folded on the floor, his trench coat hung from a nail in the wall. He lifted up his sweater, and scratched his stomach, rubbing his hands over the ridges of muscle, liking what he felt. Nash wasn't up. He could hear him in the next room. The miserable sod was groaning in his sleep, like a pregnant sow.

In stocking feet and trouser-less, he headed towards the stairs. If Nash wanted to screw her before snuffing her out, he could. But, right now, it was his turn. His cock twitched at the thought of it.

He climbed the next set of stairs. They swayed under his weight, the old timber creaking, like it was ready to snap. He'd be glad when they were out of this dump. It was a death trap. Still, it was serving its purpose; somewhere to hang out before they got rid of the antiques, away from prying eyes. His flat wouldn't have done; too many nosy neighbours. He'd split from there a few weeks ago, so the trail would be cold, if anyone came looking. Nash had done likewise.

There were no worries, though; that fog had been a Godsend. No one had seen them, not a soul. He grinned. *Not a soul who would live to tell the tale, anyway.*

He had fastened the door handle of their room by a piece of rope tethered to an adjacent door handle. Now, he untied it, and opened the door. A swathe of dismal light cut into the blackness of the room. There was a fragrance in the air. He'd expected to smell piss and shit, like they'd crapped themselves.

The woman and her kid scrambled even closer to each other, like a couple of frightened mice. Then, she got to her feet, shielding the kid behind her. He could tell they'd both been crying, and neither looked like they'd slept a wink.

"Good morning," he said, and gave them both the benefit of his smile.

The woman's eyes flicked over him, resting briefly on the bulge in his underpants. He saw her cringe.

"Care to stretch your legs, beautiful?" he asked pleasantly.

"You're letting us go?"

"Now, that all depends on whether you do as I say, and you don't give me any grief." He extended his arm for her to go with him. As they both made a move, he held up his hand. "Ladies, one at a time."

She jerked backwards, as she grasped his meaning. "You keep away from us."

He inclined his head, so his blond hair flopped over one eye. He guessed he must look pretty good to her. "So, you don't want to go home?"

"Of course we do."

She really did look like a little mouse, cowering there, short tousled hair, big frightened eyes, but in a way, he quite admired her guts. For a woman, she had balls. All the other women he'd known in his life would have shit themselves by now. He kept his tone pleasant. "And you will, but all in good time. I thought we might have a little chat first. Get to know one another. What do you say?"

She drew back, almost as if she were drawing back into her skin. "Let us go. Please. I swear we won't say anything…" her voice broke. "You have my word."

Her voice was beginning to remind him of Nash's—whining, whinging, but there, the resemblance ended. She was good looking, slim, although he couldn't really tell, since she had a coat on. He was quite looking forward to finding out.

"Well, let's you and me go and talk about that, shall we? I'd suggest you leave the kid here. Grown up stuff isn't for the likes of kiddies, is it?" He saw the colour drain from her pale face, and she swore at him.

He held the door open, addressing the child clinging to her mother. "Ignore Mummy's little outburst." Then, to her, he said, "You really oughtn't to swear in front of little ones. It's not nice. Now, are you coming, or shall I take the kid? It's your choice."

For a minute, she didn't move. She stood there, white-faced, while the kid clung onto her, crying again. He folded his arms, patiently. Then, as he was about to reach for the kid, she prised herself free.

"Mummy, don't go!" the kid yelled.

"It's all right, I won't be long. I want you to think nice thoughts, until I get back," she told her, kissing the top of her head. She walked with her nose in the air past him and out of the door, like some prissy martyr.

He followed her, fastening the rope to the door handles after him. The kid started to bawl again.

Vincent turned to face her on the dismal passageway. There was terror in her eyes. It elated him, thrilled him. He couldn't wait. "Downstairs, gorgeous."

She didn't argue, but walked stiffly down the rickety staircase to the floor below. He directed her along to his room, kicking the door shut after them.

She was trembling. Her whole body was literally shaking, and her skin was like chalk. She stood, not screaming, not clawing him, not trying to get away. It was as if she was accepting her fate, like some sacrificial lamb.

He stood facing her, looking down at her, but she avoided his eyes. He gripped the zipper of her coat, and pulled it down slowly, all the time watching her face. He dragged the coat off her, and threw it in the corner. She was wearing a blue fluffy sweater, jeans, and ankle boots. She looked good—definitely shaggable. He squeezed her breast, expecting her to lash out at him. But, she remained still, except for her trembling. "You don't have to look so terrified. If you relaxed a bit, you might even enjoy yourself."

She remained mute, head turned aside. It was beginning to irritate him. She was like a fucking statue. *Why the hell hadn't she begged for mercy? Why wasn't she pleading with him to be gentle? Well, he'd get a reaction out of her, one way or the other. This was Vincent Webb screwing her, for Christ sakes. The cow ought to be grateful.*

Chapter 12

Julia had lost track of how long the ordeal lasted. She knew she'd made it worse for herself by not showing any reaction. So he'd taken his anger and frustrations out on her brutally. When he finally drew away from her, her left eye refused to open, her head throbbed, and her ribs felt broken. But, she could stand, and she got dizzily to her feet. She could still hold up her head, although she avoided looking at him, the defiance she'd felt at first now shrivelled to nothing. But, she could still think.

She dragged her clothes back into place, wiped the blood from her mouth. Every movement hurt. He watched her with loathing, then snarled at her to stay put, while he went to the bathroom. She hadn't expected to be left alone, but the second he was out of the room, she moved swiftly. Despite the pain, and the disgusting feeling of violation, she dipped into the pockets of his trench coat. When her fingers touched her car keys, she clutched at them swiftly, hiding them down her pants. She was putting her coat on, when he returned.

He got into the rest of his clothes, and Julia held her breath, in case he felt in his pockets for the keys. He only checked for his knife, then sneered, "And how was it for you, darling?"

She wanted to scream, and fly at him with fists and nails, but there was no fight left in her. Besides, she was no match for him, and she would come off worse. She swallowed back the feelings of repulsion and hatred, and said nothing. He grabbed her arm, and shoved her through the doorway, frog-marching her back upstairs. She prayed to God she wasn't too frightful a sight for Lucy.

When she reached the top floor, the horror of what she had gone through was instantly forgotten. The rope fastening the door was loose, and it stood ajar. Finding the strength from somewhere, she flung Vincent's hand off, and ran the last few steps into the room.

"Lucy!"

Two faces turned to look at her. Lucy's, thank God, still alive, kneeling on the bare floorboards. But, next to her, crouched Nash.

Julia swiftly took in the scene, thankful to see he wasn't touching her, wasn't harming her. She swept her daughter up into her arms, gasping at the pain in her ribs, but not releasing the hold she had on her child. Lucy's arms clung tightly around her neck. Tears of relief scalded her cheeks.

"Your face, Mummy…"

"It's alright, Lucy, love, it's alright." Julia's lips were pressed into Lucy's hair, breathing in her scent. "It's not as bad as it looks."

"You're a horrible man!" Lucy shrieked, her voice high pitched and distraught.

"Don't, sweetheart," Julia breathed, afraid Vincent would vent his anger on her daughter next. She inched away from them, and noticed for the first time, as the dull grey light from the passageway filled their cramped confines, what an absolute pigsty and death trap they had spent the night in.

Black mould covered the walls. The window was boarded up from the outside, although a crack in the wood allowed a streak of watery sunlight in. The glass itself was splintered into sharp jagged shards. And, to her horror, she saw the floorboards beneath the window were non-existent, she could see straight down to the floor below, and another hole in the ceiling allowed her to look into what was probably an attic. She silently thanked God neither she nor Lucy had fallen through in the night as they'd shuffled about, needing somewhere to relieve themselves, and somewhere else to lie down.

They'd slept fitfully, after feeling about and finding a box full of old bedding. Fumbling in the darkness, she had made a makeshift bed for them on the floor; it was better than hard floorboards for

Lucy. They'd cuddled close, with Lucy's blanket over the pair of them, and she'd tried not to think of their comfortable beds back home, where they were safe.

"Did we disturb you, Nash?" Vincent asked so politely Julia wanted to scream.

Nash struggled to his feet. He looked a mess. His arm must have bled again during the night, as the bandages were dark red. His eyes were sunken, and his lips almost white—like a dying man. Julia placed Lucy carefully down, holding her hand tightly, as she turned her glittering eyes to Vincent, "This man is ill, can't you see that? Are you so totally callous you'd let him rot?"

Vincent grinned, and slid an arm around the thinner man's shoulders. "Nash's okay, he doesn't look his best first thing in the mornings, do you, mate?"

Nash attempted a smile. It was pathetic. "Yeah, I'm okay," he slurred, wiping his good arm across his mouth.

Julia saw the glint of malice in the bigger man's face, and despised him totally. It was obvious to her he didn't care if his accomplice lived or died. *So why couldn't Nash see that for himself?*

And where did that leave her and Lucy? She had to keep on. Perhaps she could drive a wedge between them, split them apart, and alienate Vincent. Get Nash on their side.

"Listen to me," Julia said, forcing herself to look into Nash's face. "He wouldn't give a damn, if you dropped dead on the floor. Surely you can see that for yourself. If he cared one jot about you, he'd have let you go to hospital. I think he wants you dead…"

"Shut it!" Vincent snapped, taking a step towards her.

She held her ground, pleading with Nash. "Think about it. With you gone, there would be one less to point the finger at him over whatever you've done."

"I'm warning you," Vincent hissed, his pale eyes narrowing into slits.

Aware she was riling him, Julia kept on, driving home her point. "I don't care what you've done, but if there was money involved, he won't have to share it with you if you die, will he?"

"I said shut it!" Vincent snarled, slapping the side of her head with the flat of his hand, sending her staggering back into the wall. Lucy screamed. He turned to Nash. "Now! Do it now!"

The injured man took a faltering step nearer to her, and icy cold fear clutched Julia's heart. They meant to kill them. She could see it in their faces. The intention was so tangible, she could taste it in her dry mouth. Shielding her daughter, she searched frantically around for some kind of defence, some kind of weapon. There was nothing within reach. A broken chair, cardboard boxes filled with old clothes and books. There was nothing she could use to defend herself, or her daughter.

Her thoughts flew to Ian, hating him, loving him. Hating herself for dragging Lucy from the safety of her bed, and inflicting this terror on her.

Both men were staring at them. The bigger one, scarlet with fury, the other one, grey and sickly. For a moment, no one moved. Then, Nash shook his head slowly from side-to-side, swore softly, and dragged himself out of the room.

Vincent remained glaring, his breathing was heavy, his chest rising and falling rapidly. But, now, there was uncertainty in his face. As if he'd expected his accomplice to have acted, followed his orders, instead of walking away.

Julia saw the dilemma in his bleak eyes, and prepared herself to fight as savagely as she could. Her thoughts raced, she knew where to kick him for the maximum effect. If she could put him out of action, for a few seconds, it might be long enough to get her and Lucy away.

But, rather than attack, he moved back, towards the door, he stood to one side, so they could get past. Finally, he rasped, "Move!"

"Mummy…" Lucy wailed, clinging to her waist.

"And shut that kid up, or I will!"

Julia hugged her, trying not to cry out from the pain in her ribs. She pressed her lips against Lucy's forehead. "Please, darling, please don't cry."

But, the child wouldn't be silenced. Sobbing hysterically, she wailed, "I want my daddy... I want my daddy..."

Tears streaming down her own cheeks now, Julia cradled her child against her breast, stifling Lucy's sobs with her body.

Grabbing her elbow, Vincent shoved her roughly towards the stairs. "I said, move it!"

The floorboards groaned, and Julia felt the entire staircase sway beneath them, almost on the verge of collapse, as they stumbled down the stairs. Somehow, they reached the comparative safety of the downstairs hallway, without the stairs smashing down with them. In the kitchen, Nash was slumped down at the table, a kettle of water was coming to the boil on the paraffin stove.

She longed to sit down herself. She hurt so much from where he had savagely punched her, and violated her. She could still smell him; she felt so dirty and defiled, she could have scrubbed her skin off. She tried to block out her thoughts, tried not to dwell on the horror of his attack, but it was impossible. She could still feel his vileness inside her, his hands molesting her, the pain. She wanted to be sick, and she wanted to lash out at him. She clung onto her anger, glad of it, feeling it giving her strength. She wasn't going to be beaten. Lucy needed her, and she needed to be alert, ready to make her move when an opportunity arose.

Daylight streaked in through the grime of the kitchen window. She thought of Ian, and her eyes fluttered shut. *Had he rung her sister? Were the police out looking for them? Oh, Ian please...*

"Breakfast would be nice, don't you think?" Vincent suggested, the blazing fury, of moments ago, miraculously gone.

Julia stared at him in disbelief. *He could rape, beat, and terrorise a woman, and then, eat?* He was a psychopath. A maniac. She knew now for sure there would be no reasoning with him.

"What do you fancy, Nash, a couple of fried eggs? I'm sure our beautiful guest would be only too happy to cook for us."

The thought of food worsened her nausea, but Lucy had to be hungry. Back home, she was always ravenous at breakfast time. Back home...

The desolation and hopelessness of their situation hit her suddenly, and her knees buckled. Only the sudden tightening of Lucy's arms stopped her from collapsing. She had to be strong for her daughter's sake. She forced a smile at Lucy. It hurt when she smiled. "I bet you're hungry, sweetheart," she said, trying to sound normal for Lucy's sake. "Sit down, love, and I'll cook some eggs."

"No!" the child screamed, clinging on to her fiercely.

"It's alright, I promise," she said, looking Vincent straight in the eye. "I'm sure the man isn't going to hurt us. He wants to eat, and he wants me to cook. I can't do that if he hurts me again, can I?"

Vincent's lip curled, but it was he who turned away first. Nash began plucking at his bandages.

Irritated, Vincent dragged out a chair, and straddled it. "Cut the crap, and get on with it. There's eggs and coffee."

She poured her daughter a mug of milk, and herself a mug of water. They both drank quickly, before anyone decided to knock them out of their hands. Then, Julia began untying the knots in Nash's sling. "I'm dressing his arm first." To Nash, she said, "You've lost more blood during the night."

"You're telling me," Nash slurred. "It's been killing me, couldn't sleep."

Julia could sense Vincent's anger at Nash's needs being catered for before his. It pleased her.

She set Lucy to work sorting out the lengths of ripped shirt for bandages. Her voice lowered to a whisper, she murmured, "Did Nash touch you or hurt you, darling while I was gone?"

The child shook her head. "No, we were only talking."

"What about?"

"His little baby brother - he drowned in the bath..."

"I thought I told you it's rude to whisper?" Vincent's voice rasped out.

Julia's eyes narrowed towards him, but she bit back her response. There was no point in risking another beating. She moved to Nash, and unwound the stained rags from his arm. Her stomach churned at the sight. His flesh was raw and angry, the wound festering.

He groaned, and ran his good hand through his blood-stiffened hair. "Fuck me! Look at the state of it!"

"Haven't you any antiseptic?" Julia demanded, looking at Vincent. "Anything? Alcohol, even? This is getting infected. He needs antibiotics. He'll get blood poisoning."

"Lordy, Lordy! Listen to her. Anybody would think she had the hots for you, Nash."

"It's called humanity. Obviously, you wouldn't know."

"It doesn't look like that, from where I'm sitting," Vincent sneered. "Here, Nash, looks like you don't have to go to California to get the birds. You've got one right here."

Nash tried to smile, and failed miserably.

"You just don't care, do you?" Julia said, trembling with anger and disgust for the man.

Vincent's lips parted into one of his dazzling smiles, but this one didn't make the grade. "Course I care about my old mate. Now, get a move on and finish him, then make our breakfast, like a good girl."

Julia turned her back on him, despising him. She whispered to Nash, as she began to clean up the wound with a piece of rag and boiled water. "Watch him. He wants you out of the way."

"If I have to tell you once more about whispering..." Vincent warned. "So, what's she telling you Nash? Not trying to seduce you, is she?"

The wretch of a man tried to laugh. The attempt was pathetic. Stomach churning, Julia tried to clean the wound, trying not to heave at the sight of the puss-oozing flesh. He couldn't keep still. The pain was making his knees jerk, and his other hand bang down on the table time and again. Somehow, she tried to keep her voice steady, tried not to gag. "I'm sorry. I'm being as gentle as I can."

To her surprise, Lucy inched closer, and rested her hand lightly on Nash's agitated one, stopping him from thumping it against the table.

"Try thinking nice thoughts, till it's over," Lucy said, managing to give him a tiny smile.

So proud of her daughter, Julia's eyes filled with tears. She cleared her throat. "Did... did you say you were going to California?"

"Yeah, for me face," he mumbled, not quite so agitated now. "Gonna see a plastic surgeon. See if he can fix me face up. Hurts like hell." A trail of saliva dribbled from the bottom corner of his mouth. He didn't notice. "People don't like looking at it much, neither."

"How did it happen?" Julia asked, swabbing his injured arm, wondering rather about this recent injury. *What had they done that resulted in his arm being ripped apart like this?* Although deep down in her heart, she guessed they'd robbed Benjamin Stanton. It was Bessie she'd heard barking. Her eyes fluttered shut in despair. Benjamin wouldn't have stood a chance against these two – and poor Bess...

Now, in daylight, she could see the injury better. There were puncture marks, bites. Bessie had put up a good fight.

Vincent uncomfortably fiddled with his mobile phone. "Spare us the gory details, Nash, mate. We haven't had our breakfast yet."

Nash winced, as Julia began bandaging him again. "Someone knifed me in a fight."

"It's a wonder you weren't killed," she remarked, deliberately sounding concerned, trying to continue to drive a wedge between these two. She tried desperately not to imagine the scene that must have taken place in Benjamin's house. She forced herself to concentrate. "That cut must have gone very deep."

"Don't worry. He didn't get away with it," Nash uttered.

"No, I imagine he didn't," Julia murmured, well able to envision the revenge he would vent on anybody who crossed him. Never in her life had she met anyone as callous as this pair.

Nash sucked in his saliva. "Nor the butcher, who was supposed to fix me up."

"Nash, shut it. I haven't eaten yet," Vincent ordered, fumbling with the coffee jar now, scattering grains on the draining board.

Julia glanced sideways at him. He looked uneasy, like he'd heard this story before, and it disturbed him. Deliberately, she pressed for more information, even though she knew she wasn't going to like what she heard. But, if it destroyed the other one's concentration, then all the better. "So, what happened to him?"

The twisted mouth curled into a sneer. "Got him, didn't I, and his missus."

"You killed them?" Julia quietly asked, repulsed, but trying not to show it.

He spoke more quietly, more to himself than to her. "There's more ways of getting your own back than killing people."

She could hardly believe what she was hearing. "You wanted revenge on the man who saved your life?"

"Look at the mess he made of me," Nash argued indignantly.

"I can imagine how you must have looked before. You probably owe your life to that surgeon. What kind of monster are you?"

Nash grunted. "It was his own fault. He could have done a better job on me. He didn't give a stuff about me, and stitched me together any old how. Bet he did a better job on his missus, after I'd seen to her. Well, not that he was in any fit state to fix anybody up." He stared straight into Julia's eyes for a moment. She saw the void where compassion should have lain, and she shuddered violently.

"You maimed her?"

He shrugged. "Followed her one night, didn't I? Had myself a Stanley knife…"

"Nash, will you pack it in," Vincent snarled, slamming his hand down on the table.

Julia didn't want to know either; the callous cold-bloodedness terrified her. Yet, she needed to understand what he was capable of. Besides, Vincent was getting agitated again, and that put him at a disadvantage in her eyes. "Lucy, put your hands over your ears, and don't listen, darling. Hum a nice song to yourself." Then, looking back at Nash, she asked, "What did you do?"

"Took her apart, didn't I, after I'd had my wicked way."

Julia's eyes closed, wanting to block out the images forming, as Nash went on in all its gory detail.

"For fuck's sake, shut it!" Vincent growled, banging his chair around. "I want to eat, not spew up."

Ignoring Vincent's outburst, Julia forced herself to keep digging for more information. "What about the surgeon, did you take him apart, too?"

"Him? Nah. I smacked his fingers a little bit. Made sure he didn't get to use them on nobody else in a hurry."

"But, you're still going to put your trust in the hands of another plastic surgeon," said Julia. "And what will you do, if you're not satisfied with the finished result, maim him, too, and his wife?"

"Nah, I'll be paying for this job, and I'll be getting meself a top-notch surgeon. And it won't be long now. Gonna have me good looks back soon."

Julia said no more, disgusted by what she'd heard, aware they were as bad as one another. They were both violent rapists. They were killers already, and she had no doubt they would think nothing of murdering her and Lucy to protect themselves. There would be no reasoning with them, no pleading for mercy. She was going to have to outwit them, or fight their way out of here, somehow.

She finished tending Nash's arm, making sure the sling was secured tightly, immobilising his arm again. "I'll get rid of these old bandages, and make breakfast."

"Nice try, beautiful," said Vincent, getting up swiftly, and barring her way. "And where were you planning on depositing them? Outside in the trash, so you could do a runner?"

Her voice was harsh. "And leave my daughter with you two?"

The perfected smile faded, and he shrugged. "Some would."

"Not me!"

Vincent's lip curled, and he patted Nash's shoulder. "We must talk, Nash. After breakfast, I think." Julia caught the look the two men exchanged, and her blood ran cold. Time was running out.

Taking the frying pan, Julia scraped the old fat they must have used yesterday, and washed the pan out. She hesitated, before adding a blob of margarine. The pan was heavy, if she could get a good enough swing, she might be able to stun one of them. *Only, what of the other man? And which one to hit first?* The clear choice would be Vincent, and it would be a pleasure to feel the cast iron smack into his skull.

She sensed him behind her, and she swung round, more in fright than anything. He caught her wrist, twisting it.

"And what were you thinking of doing?" he mused. "Why, Nash, I think your little lady friend was going to try and batter us with a frying pan."

Nash said nothing, a grunt, as if he'd talked himself out, his energy spent. Julia almost pitied him. He was in a frightful state. No, it wouldn't have been him she attacked first, had she got the chance. Despite all she'd heard of Nash's horrendous deeds, she still felt Vincent was the more dangerous of the two.

"I was about to cook your eggs," she answered flatly, wrenching her arm free of his grasp. He grinned, and her fingers itched to let fly at him.

"Don't let me stop you, then," he said, swinging his chair next to Nash, and sitting down. The pair whispered together, as she cooked.

She did the best she could with the food, taking special care with her daughter's egg and bread, although food was the last thing on her mind. She didn't know if there would be another meal. And she needed her strength, if she was to get her and Lucy out of this mess.

The kettle re-boiled, as they were eating. "A splash of milk in mine," Vincent said, his mouth full of runny egg. "Black for Nash - like his heart," he added, giving the injured man a playful punch on his good arm.

Julia made the coffee, and set them down, as Nash reached across for some bread, his arm catching his mug, spilling the scalding liquid right into Vincent's lap. He sprang up, screaming.

Reacting swiftly, and automatically, Julia moved. Grabbing Lucy's arm, she dragged the startled child to the back door, while Vincent was screaming, and tugging at his jeans. She yanked back the bolt with every ounce of strength she possessed and turned the door handle. It opened easily, and for a second, she lost her balance. As cold, damp November air blew into her face, she rallied swiftly and ran, slamming the door after them.

At first. she was dragging Lucy, until the child also tasted freedom. and raced along beside her, and then, ahead of her, pulling Julia frantically.

Behind them, she heard the back-door opening, and Vincent raging. Shooting a glance over her shoulder, she saw him stumble after her. Blindly, she and Lucy ran around the side of the house, feet slithering on a path smothered in wet, dead leaves. She fumbled for the car keys tucked down her pants, as she ran.

They reached the car and skidded around to the driver's side. Instantly, she rammed the key into the door lock and turned it. She pulled the handle. Nothing moved. Desperately, she turned the key again and heard the lock click. The door opened, and she propelled Lucy inside, falling in after her, as Vincent lurched towards them.

Lucy screamed, as he barged against the side of the car, but Julia was quicker, slamming the door, and pressing the central locking button, keeping him on the other side. His face pressed hard against the side window, contorted with pain and fury. Fumbling with the ignition key, she managed to get it in, and turn it. Nash was almost upon them, too, lurching towards them like a wounded animal.

"Please, please…" she breathed, her hand shaking, as she turned the key, her heartbeat pounding in her skull.

The engine turned over with a whining sound. Vincent banged the window with his fists, put his shoulder against the window, yanked at the handle, kicked the door furiously. The starter motor continued to turn over—whirring, whining.

"Start! Start you blasted car!" Julia screamed. "Start, please God start!"

"Mummy, make the car go," Lucy pleaded.

"It's damp. It hates the damp…" She knew it. She should have guessed. It was always difficult to make it start in the damp. "Oh God…"

The crash came so suddenly, Julia could only gasp. The side window caved in, and amid the cascade of brick and splintering glass, a hand reached through, and banged the central locking button.

Lucy began to scream.

Chapter 13

Ian had never been drunk at ten in the morning before in his life, but then again, his wife and daughter had never left him before. Amazing, really, when he thought how he'd treated her these last few months. It was a wonder she'd put up with him for this long.

Three-quarters of a bottle of scotch had done nothing for his mood, apart from making him throw up in the bathroom fifteen minutes ago. It certainly hadn't miraculously come up with any answers as to what he could say to her.

Pushing a half empty glass away in disgust, he got unsteadily to his feet. Not heading to the toilet this time, but to wherever he'd left his mobile. The room spiralled, and he grabbed the arm of the chair to steady himself. *Phone her*, he told himself. He had to ring her. Bleary-eyed, he found his mobile, and scrolled his list of contacts. Swaying and blinking, the names and numbers swam in front of his eyes.

Leaning against the wall, he caught sight of his reflection in the mirror, unshaven, and pissed out of his skull. *How the hell could he apologise to Julia in this state?* He needed a shower, and time to sober up.

As he staggered back to the sofa, he told himself this was the best option. Sleep it off, shower and freshen up, then, call her.

She'd curled herself up into a ball, lying across the kid, shielding her from his fists that pummelled into her kidneys, but there was no moving her. She'd latched herself onto her car seat. He wasn't going to waste any more energy, and his cock was burning like hell from the scald. He went around to the passenger side, hauled the door open, and dragged the screaming kid out. That was easier. And it moved the bitch. She was out in a flash, kicking and punching him. He used the kid as a shield, swinging her around, so that one of the woman's punches hit the kid in the leg.

They were both shrieking like banshees. He had to get them indoors, before someone heard them. The kid was as light as a feather, and with her arms pinned to her sides, as he carried her back into the house, she was no trouble. The fucking woman was, though. A couple of backhanders sent her reeling, but she was straight back, trying to get around to the front of him, pawing at his coat. He knew what she was after. But, if she thought he was stupid enough to let her get her hands on his Bowie, she was an idiot.

"Nash! Get your arse up here!"

For once, Nash looked like he'd got a bit of life back in him. He followed them up the two flights, not doing a fucking thing to stop the woman, though. In the bedroom, he threw the kid into the corner, onto their makeshift bed. Another back-hander sent the woman flying in that direction, too. They fell into a heap of arms and legs.

Vincent turned to Nash, Bowie knife drawn. "Now! Do it now, or I do it myself, nice and slowly."

Nash's half-dead eyes seemed to glitter, like he relished the idea. This was the Nash he knew—violent, black-hearted.

"Out my way!" Nash uttered, drawing the lump of metal from his inside pocket.

Vincent drew back, feeling sick suddenly. He didn't want to watch this. Gore wasn't his thing. The deed needed to be done, though, and quick. "Get on with it," he uttered, stepping outside the door, and slamming it shut on the three of them.

They were both shrieking now—shrieking and begging. Then, he heard a thud, a sickening sound, and the kid went silent. The woman shrieked all the more. Then, another thud, and she was silent. Two more thuds, then a third, and a forth.

Vincent could picture the scene in his head. He didn't actually want to see it with his eyes. Eventually, he inched open the door, and saw Nash throw the kid's blanket over the two bodies, the woman lying on top of the kid, like she'd done in the car, arse up in the air.

When Nash looked at him, there was a bleak emptiness in his eyes, and his shoulders slumped, as if it had taken every last drop of energy from him.

"Well done, my old mate," Vincent said, smiling, and slapping him on the back. "Thought for a minute earlier, they'd got to you, found a soft spot in that old black heart of yours."

"Maybe they did," Nash muttered, slurring, wiping the cosh on a corner of the blanket, before slipping it back inside his jacket. "But, they ain't gonna stop my plans." He met Vincent's eyes. "Nothin's gonna get in me way of getting off to California. Now, we gonna get that fucking car started, and get out of here, or what?"

Vincent smiled. This Nash he liked – well, *like* wasn't really the appropriate word, but it was better than loathing.

He closed the bedroom door, and followed Nash downstairs. "Steady how you go, matey. Bloody stairs are a death trap."

Chapter 14

It was well after mid-day when Ian finally came to properly. Nevertheless, his hand trembled, as he dialled Julia's mobile. He sat on the edge of their bed, clean-shaven now, his hair slicked back and curly from his shower. He looked vaguely human again, minus the shadows under his eyes, and the almost permanently guilty expression he wore. He practised what he would say, as he listened to the phone ringing out. But, there was another sound now, the familiar catchy sound of his wife's mobile's ring tones coming from downstairs.

"Julia?" She'd come home. She'd come quietly in while he was in the shower. Relief washed over him, only to be followed by a tightening of his stomach at the thought of facing the music. But, the desire to see her again outweighed his worries. *Coming home meant she was ready to forgive him, didn't it?* He ran down the stairs, desperate to see her and Lucy.

Her mobile was ringing in the lounge, and he dashed in, aware his heart was banging ridiculously quickly against his ribcage. "Julia..."

She wasn't in the living room at all. Nor was she in the kitchen, or the study. The rooms were exactly as he'd left them. The phone had stopped ringing.

"Julia? Where are you? Julia? Lucy?"

He redialled, waited a second, and then, heard the same ringtones. They were definitely coming from here, in the lounge. With a sinking heart, he traced the sound to the sofa. Sliding his hand down between the cushions, he fished out his wife's mobile.

For long, bleak moments, he stared at the screen, and his own face that came up with the words: *Ian calling*.

He recalled she'd taken that photo of him last spring, the morning of Lucy's eighth birthday. He'd cooked pancakes for the three of them, and Julia had kissed some drops of syrup off his lips.

He pressed his fingertips into his eye sockets to keep from weeping, waiting for the sensation to fade, and then, scrolling down to his sister-in-law's number, he dialled that.

He caught his breath, as the phone was almost immediately snatched up at the other end.

"Julia, is that you?"

"No, it's Steph… Ian? You okay? You sound slightly inebriated." There was amusement in her voice.

He wasn't aware he was frowning. He wasn't even conscious of the shiver that ran down his spine. All that registered was the fact his wife's younger sister was reacting normally toward him. She wasn't calling him all the two-timing bastards under the sun. Julia couldn't have told her.

"Ian, speak to me. Are you sloshed?"

"What?"

"Are you drunk?"

Why hadn't Julia told her? Embarrassment he guessed. "Steph, can I speak to Julia, please?"

There was a brief silence, before she answered with another chuckle. "My, you are sloshed. Julia isn't here. What made you think she would be with me?"

The last effects of the scotch lifted. He sobered instantly. "Well, because she said she was going over to your place…"

"Oh, she's probably popped into town to do a bit of retail therapy first. I'll get her to ring you when she shows up, shall I?"

"Yes… no," he babbled, his head starting to throb. "I don't mean she's left here for your place, I mean… Oh dammit, nothing, forget it."

"Are you alright, Ian? You sound a teeny bit confused. Heavy night last night, was it?"

He pressed his knuckles against his temple. *Where the devil was she, then?* But, for the time being, he wasn't in any mood to start explaining the situation to his sister-in-law. "Yeah, something like that. Don't worry, Steph. I must have got it wrong. If she happens to turn up, get her to call me, please."

"Course I will. And I'll tell her to buy a big bottle of headache tablets on the way home for your hangover."

She was expecting him to laugh, and he did his best not to disappoint her. He hung up as soon as he could, and sank down onto the sofa, both mobiles in his hands.

Where the hell was she?

He made more coffee. Waiting for the water to boil, he re-read Lucy's note to him. She seemed pretty certain that they were heading to Steph's, which meant either Julia had changed her mind at the last minute, or she'd lied to Lucy about where they were going, so that he couldn't follow. His eyes closed. God, what a complete idiot he was to have let the two people, whom he loved most in the world, slip out of his life. And all for a woman who would have happily stabbed him in the back with a pair of scissors.

He pulled the plaster from his arm. It was bad enough being stabbed in the wrist. *What if she'd stabbed him in his neck, or the groin?* The image in his mind of her lunging at him, her face all screwed up in anger, sent a chill down his spine. He hadn't thought she was that unbalanced, or as desperate to keep a hold on him. She'd clearly read more into their affair than he had realised. She might have thought it could turn into something permanent. It wasn't what he'd intended but it's possible that's what she'd hoped for.

He poured boiling water into his coffee mug, splashing it everywhere as his thoughts about Shelley cleared. It had been sex, simple as that. A bit of excitement with an older woman. *God, he was pathetic.*

Taking the coffee back through to the lounge, he slumped into a chair, as he tried to unscramble his thoughts. Julia had to have gone somewhere. There were no other relatives on her side. *Would she go to one of his?* He doubted it, somehow. They were never very close. Steph was her closest ally. It was odd she hadn't gone there. She was the most obvious person to pour all her troubles out to.

Trying to think straight, he scrolled through the contacts in her mobile, looking to see if any other names sprang to mind. He rang one of her friends, one of the mums from school. He kept his voice light, making out there wasn't a problem, just she'd said she was popping out to a friend's, but hadn't said who, and he needed to contact her, but she'd left her mobile at home. It was all very plausible.

An hour later, he'd rang everyone the pair of them knew. No one had seen her. Or, if they had, they weren't saying.

His stomach rumbled. It had been hours since he'd eaten. Going through to the kitchen, he put a wedge of cheese between two slices of bread. When his house phone rang, he was through the kitchen door in a flash, banging it back so hard against the wall the patterned glass cracked from top to bottom.

"Shit!"

He stood on a piece of Lego in his stocking feet, and hopped to the phone. Lucy was a monkey, never putting her toys away, but right then, the scattered toys brought an ache to his heart. He snatched up the phone. "Hello!"

"Well, you don't sound too sick," a male voice said.

Disappointment washed over him like a tidal wave. "Tony."

"Sounds more like you've been out jogging. How are you feeling?"

He rallied, trying to think what excuse he'd left for his boss that morning about not coming into work. For the life of him, he couldn't remember. "I wish I *could* go out jogging," he answered, racking his brains.

"Something you ate, do you reckon?"

"What?"

"The sickness and the runs. Something you ate? Has Julia come down with it, too?"

"No, she's… she's fine," he said, recalling now he'd said he'd got a stomach bug.

"Well, make sure you're okay before thinking of coming in tomorrow," said Tony Wyndham.

"I will," Ian answered, wondering if Shelley was in work, and how she was fairing after he knocked her out flat. His eyes fluttered shut at the thought of doing that to a woman. *God, he was such a sick bastard.* For all he knew, she could be still lying unconscious on her bedroom floor.

He told himself he was worrying unnecessarily. Her husband should have found her, although he didn't know if he was working away; he often did, when he had to out-source materials. Ian cleared his throat. "Is everything okay at your end? No one else off sick with a bug?"

"No," came the answer, and then, "Well, Shelley hasn't turned up, nor phoned in…"

He didn't hear any more, his ears began to buzz. Somehow, he got through the rest of the conversation, relieved when Tony hung up, wishing him a speedy recovery.

He sat for an age, imagining Shelley in a coma, dead by the time her husband returned from his trip.

"Get a bloody grip!" he said to himself. She'd be fine. But, he stared at his phone. He couldn't leave it. He knew her number by heart, but keyed in the code to hide his number. He didn't want to speak to Shelley. He needed to hear her voice, and know she was alive. It rang twice, before being answered. It was a man's voice. Ian hung up quickly, feeling like a stalker.

He guessed it was her husband. That was good. If he was around to answer her mobile, that meant he was there to look after her. Anyway, it was Julia and Lucy he had to worry about.

He finished his sandwich, barely tasting it, a dull ache starting up behind his eyes. He wondered whether Julia had found out who it was he'd been seeing. A sickly thought struck him. She could have gone to see Shelly. Spent the night in a hotel, then, gone to call on her today. *But, then, what would she do with Lucy?*

Of course! She'd be at school. He glanced at the wall clock. Two-thirty. A feeling of relief washed away the pain in his skull, and all his anxiety. He could meet up with Julia when she went to pick their daughter up.

He felt as if a great weight had been miraculously lifted from him. His appetite returned, and with a much lighter heart, he made himself another sandwich.

Chapter 15

Their bodies lay entwined beneath the blanket, Julia shielding her daughter, their heads close together. Neither of them moved, nor uttered a sound. She didn't need to tell her daughter that they had to lie still, play dead. She'd lost track of time; it could have been an hour or a few minutes ago since Vincent threw her daughter onto the floor, hit her in the face again, and yelled at Nash to kill them. He hadn't stayed to watch. He'd slammed the door on them, leaving them at the mercy of Nash.

She'd been ready to fight, as Nash had taken the length of metal from inside his jacket. But the second Vincent had left the room, Nash had mouthed two words, "Trust me."

There was something in his eyes both she and Lucy instantly saw. If she'd had more than a second to think about it, she probably wouldn't have hesitated in trying to overpower him. Now, she thanked God she hadn't kicked and pummelled him; the outcome might have been very different. So, in that split second when he'd said *trust me,* they had.

"Scream," he slurred, the word a whisper. "Then, shut it. Play dead."

Lucy screamed first. She turned her eyes to Julia, as if telling her to scream as well. She did so, and there was no pretending when Nash raised the cosh above his head. But, rather than bringing it down on them, he slammed it down onto the rumpled bedclothes. A look in Lucy's direction silenced her. He pointed the cosh at the floor. She slumped down.

Julia screamed again. He hit the floorboards again, through the old clothing. She fell silent, and slumped to the floor, lying on top of her daughter. Then wide-eyed, she and Lucy had clung to one another, watching mesmerised as he hit the floor through the woollen material, again and again. Then, he threw the blanket over them. A second later the door had opened, and Vincent was back, checking Nash had done as he was told.

Thank God he hadn't looked under the blanket. She had no doubt Nash's mercy would have condemned him to death, too, if Vincent had found out. He wouldn't have had any hesitation in slicing all three of them to ribbons, had he discovered the truth.

She didn't know how long they would have to stay like this. She only prayed the pair would get her car working, and go. But, for now, they had to stay put, not moving, not speaking – playing dead.

Chapter 16

At three-fifteen, Ian drove the half-mile to St John's Primary School. He parked a little way from the gates, not wanting Julia to see him the minute she arrived, in case she turned tail and disappeared. He switched off the engine, turned on the radio, and sat patiently.

The quiet street gradually came alive with parents and grandparents, some with infants in pushchairs, some with toddlers. They gathered in small groups around the school gates, chatting.

Ian sat upright, watching as every car turned the corner, expecting at any second to see Julia's yellow Mini. At three-thirty, the children poured out of school. Realising he must have missed her, he got quickly out, and crossed the road to the school gates. He scanned the eager little faces that came running from across the playground, bags slung over the shoulders.

"Did you find her, then?"

He spun round to find one of Julia's friends, whom he'd called earlier. She stood, patiently waiting for an answer. "Oh, er, no, she must have got waylaid in town. You know what the traffic is like this time of day. Thought I'd better come and collect Lucy, in case Julia didn't get back in time."

The young woman went to say something, but was jumped on by a curly haired boy who unloaded his bag, lunchbox, and violin onto her, before charging after his pal. She smiled instead. "Kids! See you!"

"Yes, see you," Ian answered, turning his attention back to the school entrance. The flow of children had thinned. Most now had been paired up with their parent or grandparent, and were being packed into cars, or led off down the street.

Standing in the school doorway, Ian spotted Lucy's teacher. She was telling someone still inside to hurry up. It had to be Lucy. He strode to meet her, ridiculously eager to see his daughter, but, at the same time, terrified, in case she knew how he'd hurt her mother. He stopped in his tracks as a skinny-legged boy, with carrot coloured hair, came running out, and a parent overtook him to meet the child.

The teacher was about to close the door, when she spotted Ian standing in the playground. She smiled at him. "Hello, Mr. Logan. Thank goodness that horrible fog has lifted. How is Lucy? It's such a shame she's missed school today. We picked the children to be in the nativity play, and I know your Lucy wanted to be the Angel Gabriel. I hope she's not going to be too disappointed; only, we had to choose from those available. Tell her she'll still be in the choir as an ordinary angel which is as important."

"Yes, yes, I will," he uttered, feeling sick to the soul, and aware a nerve had started ticking in his cheek.

"A cold, is it?" the teacher continued. "I've half a dozen off with coughs and sneezes."

"What, oh, yes," he agreed, deciding there was no way on this Earth he could admit to his daughter's teacher his wife and child had left him because of his adultery. Or, he hadn't the faintest idea where they were or when he'd see them again.

"Well, thank you for popping by and telling me," the teacher said, flashing him a smile. "Let's hope she's feeling better tomorrow."

He returned her smile, even managed a cheery wave, before walking back across the deserted playground. There was a hollow sensation in the pit of his stomach. *Where in God's name were they?*

He didn't drive straight home, but took a detour around the places they might be. Friends of friends' houses. Friends who he'd already rang but who might be lying at Julia's request. He drove slowly, looking for her yellow Mini. But, as darkness fell, he finally gave up and went home.

He was hungry. He opened a can of soup, and ate it straight from the saucepan, with a couple of slices of dry bread. Two more cups of coffee, and a lot more thought. Julia was an intelligent woman. It was more than possible she'd discovered who he was seeing. If so, she may have called on Shelley to find out the extent of the affair. Maybe even to tell Shelley's husband what was going on. The more he thought about it, the more positive he was that she would have spoken to Shelley by now.

He rang her again, not withholding his number this time. The same male voice answered. *Why the devil wasn't Shelley answering her own phone?*

He took a second to gather his wits. He kept his voice business-like. "Could I speak to Shelley de Main, please?"

He heard the hesitation in the man's voice. "Who is this?"

"Ian Logan. I work with Shelley," he said, trying to sound like his world wasn't falling apart. "Sorry to bother you, only I wasn't in work today, damn stomach bug, and it looks like I won't be in tomorrow either, so I thought I'd better let Shelley know, as we were half through an important project."

"You weren't in?" He sounded suspicious.

"No, I…"

"Neither was she. She…" he hesitated. "Something happened to Shelley last night. It's shaken her up pretty badly."

"Something happened?" Ian repeated, finding it suddenly hard to breathe.

The husband sighed. "Well, I may as well tell you, seeing as you work together. She was attacked."

Ian stared blindly at the wall. *She'd carried her threat through? Told him she was raped? Oh God!* "Attacked?" he managed to utter.

"Yes, some young swine snatched her bag, as she was coming out of the cinema, gave her a nasty punch on the jaw."

His eyes fluttered shut. She hadn't screamed rape. *Thank God, thank God.* Somehow, he managed to say, "That's terrible. I'm so sorry to hear that. Can… can I speak to her?"

De Main paused. "Hold on, she's in bed. I'll take the phone up to her." He chatted. as he huffed and puffed up the stairs. "I thought I'd bring it downstairs so she could get some rest. Damn thing never stops ringing."

Ian heard the bedroom door open, and could imagine the cream carpet, the red silk sheets, Shelley propped up on pillows in one of her flimsy negligees. Guilt swamped him again.

"Shelley, love. Someone on the phone for you," Ian heard the husband say. "Someone you work with. Ian somebody."

There was a pause, a silence, and he realised then what a position he'd landed her in. She'd clearly had to lie about being slapped in the face. She hadn't put him in the frame, and now, here he was, calling her up, expecting her to tell him if she'd had a visit from Julia – with the husband looking on.

When she came on the line, her voice sounded clipped. "Hello?"

He felt his nerves tighten. "Shelley… your husband has told me what happened. I'm so sorry to hear that. How are you feeling?"

There was no hiding the bitterness, nor the fact her husband was right beside her. "I'm feeling furious, if you must know. If I get my hands on the bastard who hit me, I'll make him pay."

The threat was levelled at him, but he replied the only way possible with a third party listening in. "Quite right. It's not safe to walk the streets these days," he said, hesitating. "Um, the reason I'm calling was to ask if you'd had a visitor today."

"Who?" she asked, her voice irritated and curt.

He could hardly tell her with her husband eavesdropping. He hoped Shelley grasped the gist of what he was trying to say. "The Julia woman – but you haven't been in the office, and she'd hardly call round to your home, would she?"

"I've not been at the office, so I've no idea," Shelley snapped. "I have to go, I've a wretched migraine."

"Yes, I'm sorry, really sorry, Shelley." He put the phone down, and slumped down into an armchair, head in his hands. In a way, he pitied Shelley, having to string a pack of lies to her husband to explain away the bruise he'd given her. He shouldn't have hit her so hard. On the one hand, she was coming at him with scissors, but he could have gotten them off her, without hitting her. He felt sick. They didn't come much worse than him.

Chapter 17

Vincent slammed the bonnet of the Mini down, and kicked viciously at the wing. "Fucking piece of shit!"

He'd spent hours trying to get it working. Now, the battery was as dead as a dodo, and he was frozen to the marrow.

Storming into the house, he found Nash slumped, head down on the table, the paraffin stove lit, and the kettle boiling. A half mug of coffee was next to his elbow. After the freezing cold of outside, it was warm in the kitchen. Vincent felt the rage building up inside. He'd been stuck out there, trying to get the car going, while Nash was warm and comfortable in here.

He wanted to kick the chair from under the moron, and knock his head into next week. But, he wasn't stupid. Somehow or other, Nash had hidden reserves of strength to call on when he needed them. No point now in getting into a fight with him. A crack on the head with that cosh of his, as well as a scalded dick, was the last thing he needed.

He glared at the back of Nash's head, despising the ugly sod more and more with every second he had to spend with him.

This was all going wrong. They should have gotten rid of the stuff by now, and gone their separate ways. *Fucking car!* Now, they were stuck out here, in the middle of nowhere, with no way of getting to London to offload what they'd nicked.

Stupid fucking woman! She deserved to die for driving a wreck that wouldn't start.

He made himself a coffee, warming his hands on the cup as he sipped it.

Nash came groggily awake. He sat up, then started rocking back and forth. "Me arm kills, Vince."

Hatred bubbled under the surface; he kept it hidden, cracking a joke. "Never a truer word said, mate. Your arm certainly did kill. You did a good job up there earlier. I'm proud of you."

"I ain't proud of nothin'," Nash groaned. "Can we get going now?"

Vincent ruffled the other man's hair, but it was hard not to grab a handful, and twist his scrawny head backwards, until his neck snapped. "We have a bit of a problem, I'm afraid. Car's dead as a fucking dodo."

Nash's eyes rolled up into his head. "Ah, no!"

"Ah, yes, unfortunately," said Vincent, finding the radio station on his mobile phone again. He turned up the volume, as the four o'clock news came on. They both listened silently, expecting to hear something about the discovery of the old bloke. Still nothing. If only they'd got a vehicle, they'd have massive head start on the law – *if* they had a vehicle.

"We're going to have to nick another car, Nash. Reckon you could do it tonight?"

"Where from?" he groaned. "Anyhow, how can I drive one-handed."

Vincent's hands curled into fists, he relaxed them instantly. "Then, it looks like I'll have to go and find us a vehicle then, doesn't it?"

"Sorry, Vince."

"And while I'm gone, get that mess upstairs cleared away."

Nash looked blankly at him.

Vincent spoke calmly and slowly to him, so the moron would understand. "Nash, when they bulldoze this house, probably someone will take a look around first, to make sure there's no one squatting."

"Okay, got it," Nash slurred. "I'll bury them. No one will find them."

"Do it," Vincent snapped. "Have it done by the time I get back. Think you can manage that?"

"Sure thing, Vince. I won't let you down."

"Pleased to hear that," said Vincent, playfully punching the other man's misshapen chin. "*So* pleased!"

Nash dragged himself up from the chair. His groggy demeanour made Vince wonder if the bitch was right. Maybe Nash would be dead by the time he got back, and things would start to look up.

Chapter 18

Someone was ringing his doorbell. Ian jumped to his feet, then stopped himself from running to answer it. He'd practically broken his neck last time by not looking where he was going. The kitchen door was certainly going to need replacing, or at least the glass panel. Anyway, it wouldn't be Julia ringing to be let in. She'd have her key.

Opening the door, he was surprised to find the paper-boy standing there. The young teenager, face half hidden inside a hooded coat, handed him the evening newspaper, which struck Ian as odd. It was only around Christmas paper-boys would knock customer's doors, hoping for a tip. He used to do it himself, many moons ago.

"Thought I'd better tell someone," the boy said. "And you're next on my round, so thought I'd better tell you."

"Tell me what?" Ian asked irritably, wanting to shut the door on this unnecessary annoyance. All he wanted was to get down to some serious thinking about where Julia and Lucy could have got to. "Go on then, spit it out. What have you got to tell me?"

The teenager jerked his thumb over his shoulder in the direction of Benjamin Stanton's place. "The old fella's milk is still on the doorstep. It's a bit weird, because he always takes it in. He might be sick, or something."

Ian sighed. "He's forgotten, more likely."

The paper-boy didn't move. "Someone ought to check on him. He is knocking on a bit."

"Yes, okay, son. I'll check on him," Ian agreed, moving to close the door, while he fetched his coat.

The boy shifted uncomfortably. "You will go over, won't you? If he's lying hurt…"

"Yes, I'll go and check, okay? Now go on, finish your paper round."

With a backward glance at Benjamin's house, the boy walked off.

Ian closed the door, then took his coat from the peg. It was drizzling again, and almost dark. It was a rotten night. He hoped Lucy and Julia were all right. He hoped they were somewhere warm and comfortable.

A wall of tall Leylandii trees formed a hedge between Benjamin's house and his, and Ian circumvented them to reach the driveway. There was a light on in one of the bedrooms, but the downstairs was in darkness. The curtains were drawn shut. If it wasn't for the morning's milk still on the doorstep, everything would have looked normal.

Stepping up to the porch, Ian pressed his thumb against the front door bell, and listened for footsteps, or the dog barking. There were no sounds coming from inside—no TV, or anything. He rapped the knocker loudly, which usually made Bessie bark—silence. He wondered whether Benjamin had gone away for a few days, him and his dog, visiting relatives. Possibly the old chap had forgotten to cancel his milk. Julia would know… only he couldn't speak to Julia. If only he could.

He stooped down, and lifted the letterbox flap. At first, he couldn't make out anything in the darkness. However, as his eyes became accustomed, he saw there was a something on the floor near the lounge doorway. He made out the shape of the old collie, and it appeared she was sleeping, because he could vaguely make out a slight movement of her breathing. But, then, he spotted another shape on the floor by the stairs, and the hairs on the back of his neck stood on end. He could distinctly make out a slippered foot, twisted at a painful angle.

"Benjamin!" he shouted through the letterbox. "Are you okay? Can you hear me?" There was no movement, and Ian stood up, trying the door. It wouldn't open. He stooped down again. "I'm calling an ambulance, Benjamin. Help's coming. You'll be okay, my friend." He straightened, feeling dizzy with panic. The poor old chap must have fallen down the stairs. *God! How many more things were going to happen?* It was like his world had gone mad. He felt for his mobile, cursing as he realised it was back in the house. He tried to run, but his legs felt like jelly. Heart hammering with panic, he stumbled back home.

His house phone was ringing. Julia, it had to be her, He snatched it up. "Julia?"

"You've got a bloody nerve!"

The venom in the female voice made him stagger. "Who's this? Get off the line. I've got to call an am…"

"You're despicable! Unbelievable!"

"Shelley…"

"How dare you ring me," she uttered, her voice thick with malice and spite. "My husband was standing there, listening. He wanted to know what we were talking about. God, if I haven't had to spin enough lies, because of you. You know, he called the police. They questioned me for a whole hour about being mugged. An hour! Where I was attacked, what did he look like, what was he wearing, where had I been, who with, what film did I see…"

"Shelley, I'm sorry, only, please get off the line, I need to ring an ambulance, my neighbour has had an accident…"

"Spare me the details. I've got quite enough on my plate, because of you. Now, get this straight, Ian Logan. Don't you ever ring me at home again. If my husband suspects anything, I've had it. And he's all I have left right now. I'm not about to lose everything, over a pathetic swine like you."

His hand was trembling. "Shelley, I'm hanging up. It's an emergency."

She started to say something, but he cut her off. He hoped the old chap wasn't dead. He snatched up the receiver again, but there was no dialling tone. She hadn't hung up. "Shelley, hang the blasted phone up!" Then, slamming it down again, he ran through to the lounge and found his mobile. Before he'd had chance to dial, the sound of a siren outside sent him running to the window.

A police car had pulled up in the street, and the paper-boy was hopping from one foot to the other by Benjamin's driveway. Two police officers got out of the vehicle. They all hurried up the drive, and disappeared behind the trees.

The paper-boy must have flagged down the police car for it to have got here so quickly, thank God. They'd be able to break in, and get an ambulance. He hoped the old boy was okay – and the dog. Funny how she didn't wake up when he shouted through the letterbox. Old and deaf, he guessed.

Within minutes, there were more sirens, more police and an ambulance. Ian watched from his front window, thinking how surreal everything was becoming, as his neighbourhood suddenly changed from being a quiet, little cul de sac to a scene from an American gangster film. The street was teeming with emergency vehicles, even an RSPCA van, their flashing lights making patterns on his walls.

He went upstairs to get a better view, seeing other neighbours standing in their doorways and in little groups on the pavement. As he watched, he kept a look out for Julia's Mini coming down the road, stupidly thinking this commotion would bring her back home. But, the only vehicles that came were more police cars. *God, where was she?* This was insane.

Eventually, he went downstairs intending to ring Steph, and tell her he was worried about Julia and Lucy. If she knew the truth, she'd have some idea where they might have gone.

Before he reached the phone, however, someone rang his doorbell. Cursing softly, he opened the door to find two men standing on his doorstep. Judging by their manner and stance, they were plain clothes police officers, and for a second, Ian felt a stab of fear, in case they'd come to tell him something bad about his wife and daughter. And then, he jerked back to reality. It would be to do with Benjamin next door. His domestic problems were of no interest to anyone, except himself.

The shorter, older of the two officers, wearing a bulky sheepskin jacket, introduced himself as Chief Inspector O'Ryan, and his taller younger colleague as Detective Inspector Grimes.

"Sorry to disturb you, sir," said O'Ryan. "But, we'd like a word, if it's no trouble."

Ian hesitated briefly, then moved aside. As the two police officers strolled through to his lounge, he sensed their disapproval at the state of the place, and the half empty whisky bottle sitting on the coffee table.

"How is the old chap?" Ian asked. "I gather it's not good, judging by the commotion going on. He's not dead, is he?"

O'Ryan shot Ian an unsettling look, that made him again think they were here for some personal reason, not a courtesy call, or whatever this was. The Chief Inspector looked about forty-five, with tight curly black hair – what there was of it, as his receding hairline reached halfway across his head. The skin on the bald area was shiny with drizzle.

"What makes you think anyone's dead, sir?" he asked, his bushy eyebrows arching, and his small round eyes taking everything in, making instant judgements.

"Well, because he was lying at the foot of the stairs."

"How do you know that, Mr. Logan? You are Ian Logan, aren't you?"

"Yes," Ian murmured. The fact this policeman knew his name sent alarm bells clanging in his mind. "I caught a glimpse of him, when I peeped through the letterbox."

They were both regarding him curiously, waiting for him to tell more.

"The kid… the paper-boy told me Benjamin's milk was still on his doorstep. He wanted me to check on him."

"I see, sir," said O'Ryan. "You saw the gentleman lying at the foot of his stairs, and you didn't think to call an ambulance?"

"Of course I did," Ian exclaimed, finding this whole thing ridiculous. "I came straight back here, and…"

"And made the call?" asked the other officer, Grimes, writing everything down in his notebook.

Ian's throat felt tight, like he was making excuses. "No, I didn't get chance. My phone was ringing when I got back in, and I couldn't get rid of the person on the line – well, not until I hung up. And even then, she was still there. She hadn't hung up, so I grabbed my mobile to ring from that, when I heard you lot arriving. So, there was no point then." He turned towards Grimes. "And why are you writing down everything I'm saying?"

"Just routine, sir," said the younger officer.

"Well, Mr. Logan," said Chief Inspector O'Ryan. He spoke slowly, steadily, while the expression in his eyes warned his brain was working at a much swifter pace, analysing and processing information, and making quick assumptions. "As you've probably gathered, a particularly nasty incident has occurred next door to you."

"Hold on," Ian said, holding his hands up. "What's that supposed to mean? A nasty incident? Benjamin's fallen down the stairs, hasn't he?"

The two officers glanced at one another, making Ian feel as if they didn't buy his question. He was starting to feel light-headed. Something here wasn't right. "Yes, okay, falling downstairs is nasty…"

"It is, sir," said O'Ryan. "Especially when it results in a death."

Ian felt his legs go weak, he took a few steps backwards, and slumped down on the arm of his sofa. "Ah, Jesus. That's a rotten shame. Poor old chap. My wife's going to take this pretty badly."

"Close were you, sir?" asked O'Ryan.

"Just neighbourly, you know. My wife gets his shopping, and does a few jobs for him. That sort of thing."

"Is she around, sir?"

He kept his eyes down. "No, not at the moment."

"When will she be back?"

Ian shook his head. "I've no idea."

There was a pause, and without looking, Ian knew the two were exchanging looks again, making assumptions. His personal life had nothing to do with them.

"So, you tried to call an ambulance from your hall phone," said Grimes, wandering through to the hall. "After you'd spotted the gentleman lying at the foot of his stairs?"

"Yes. I said so. Only someone rang me, and wouldn't get off the line."

Out in the hall, Ian heard the younger officer picking up his phone. "Seems fine now, Mr. Logan."

Ian couldn't believe their stupidity. *Weren't they listening to a word he was saying?* "Well, of course it is now!" he snapped. "What the hell do you take me for? Do you think I'd let the poor soul lie there…"

"We're not thinking anything yet, sir," said O'Ryan. "Just trying to make sense of a rather unpleasant situation."

Their attitude was making him feel hot under the collar, and he found himself rubbing his clammy hands down his trouser legs. He tried to keep cool, not let them rile him. He took a steadying breath. "As I said, when I heard the sirens, and saw the police, I assumed they would take it from there. No point in making an emergency call, if you've already arrived, is there?"

"Absolutely, and as you say, we have indeed taken it from there." Chief Inspector O'Ryan smiled as he spoke, but there was no warmth in the smile, and the calculating stare was back with a vengeance. "Luckily, the paper-boy flagged a passing police car down. He said he was concerned about one of his elderly customers who hadn't taken their milk in from this morning. Said he'd informed a neighbour, but didn't think the neighbour was going to do anything about it. I gather that was you, Mr. Logan?"

Ian's face was burning, as he defended himself. "Yes, I imagine it was, but I did do something, I went straight round there, and saw the situation for myself…"

"Then, came home, and had a conversation about something quite different," Grimes interrupted, speaking from out in the hallway. "Who was on the phone, sir? It says your last caller withheld their number."

"That doesn't surprise me," Ian murmured, beginning to feel like he was on trial here. "And I'm sure the message that says the number was withheld will also tell you what time they called, which will tally with what I'm telling you… but why the hell I should be explaining all this to you, I don't know."

"You're helping us with our enquiries, Mr. Logan," O'Ryan said pleasantly. "It wouldn't hurt to tell us who called you, would it?"

Ian's mouth dropped. "Helping you with your enquiries? What the hell is that supposed to mean?"

Grimes wandered back into the lounge, pencil and notebook poised. "Who called you, Mr. Logan? Your wife?"

Ian was about to protest. They had no reason to question him like this, but the sharp-eyed stare from the Chief Inspector shot down his resolve. Quietly, he said, "No, it wasn't my wife. It was a work colleague."

"Their name, sir?"

He took a deep breath, aware he was hammering another nail into Shelley's coffin. "Shelley de Main."

"And her number, if you wouldn't mind?"

He told them, getting to his feet, stunned by all the questions. Grimes went back into the hall and called her. The conversation that took place shook Ian to the core, as he realised Shelley was denying any such conversation ever took place, branding him a liar.

The lanky police officer regarded him with a deeply troubled frown etched across his thin face. "Shelley de Main says the last time she spoke to you was this afternoon. She was quite adamant about it."

"Now, why would she lie, sir?" asked the broader officer, unbuttoning his sheepskin, as if he was settling in for the night. "Why would she lie?"

Ian pressed his fingers against his temples, as his head ached and buzzed. "Because she hates my guts."

O'Ryan sat down beside him on the sofa. The proximity was much too close for comfort. "And why does she hate your guts, Mr. Logan?"

"Personal reasons."

"Are you married, Mr. Logan?" asked O'Ryan. "Oh, yes, you said your wife runs errands for the deceased. And she's not at home at the moment."

Ian shook his head, staring down at the carpet through his fingers.

"So, when is she likely to be back?"

"I told you, I've no idea."

"None at all?"

"No! No idea at all. She's left me, alright?" He snatched up the whisky bottle, and poured himself a tumbler full.

The two officers glanced at each other, then Grimes asked, "Are you sure it wasn't your wife on the telephone?"

Ian looked from one officer to the other. Their damning appraisals sent alarm bells began clanging in his head. "No, it wasn't my wife. I'd have told you if it was my wife. Why the hell would I lie? What the devil are you getting at?"

O'Ryan arched his bushy eyebrows. "We're not getting at anything. Just piecing it all together, that's all."

"Well, this bit of the jigsaw has nothing to do with Benjamin falling down the stairs." He took a gulp of whisky, and coughed as it burnt the back of his throat. "And I'm pretty damn sure with technology being what it is, you can find out who my last caller was, and you'll see I'm telling the truth."

"I've no doubt," the Chief Inspector said agreeably, and then spotted the plaster on his finger. "I see you've hurt yourself, sir. How did that happen?"

"This?" His mind raced. He didn't want to drag Shelley any deeper into this. Besides, she would only deny it. "It's nothing. I was a bit clumsy clearing up some broken glass." As he moved, his cuff slid further up his arm.

O'Ryan was quick in catching sight of the plaster on his wrist. "What's this, another cut?"

Ian pulled his sleeve down. "As I said, I was a bit clumsy. I've had a lot on my mind recently."

"Ah, yes, what with your wife leaving you," said O'Ryan, sounding very much like he didn't believe him.

Ian's cool deserted him. He slammed the glass back on the coffee table, splashing the whisky everywhere. "Look, what's all this about? I'm getting the feeling I'm being accused of something here."

"Not at all, sir," said O'Ryan. "It's our job to check things out, make enquiries, to see if anyone has seen or heard anything suspicious in the last forty-eight hours, or so."

"Suspicious? In what way? Benjamin had an accident, didn't he?" He shot swift looks from one officer to the other, a blackness starting to swamp him. Police don't come asking question because someone had fallen down the stairs. "Are you telling me someone pushed Benjamin downstairs?"

"It's hard to say, at this moment in time," said O'Ryan.

"But, why would you even think that a possibility?"

"Because, sadly, it would appear someone broke into Benjamin Stanton's house, ransacked it, killing the old gentleman in the process and half-killing his dog."

Ian sank to the floor, his legs totally giving way on him. "My God! Oh, my God."

O'Ryan and Grimes helped him onto the sofa. His head was spinning at the horror of it all. No wonder they were questioning people. No wonder people were under suspicion. He put his head in his hands. "Poor old soul. How could anyone attack a frail, helpless old man? Oh, my God, Julia's going to be heartbroken." He lifted his eyes to them. "And his dog? Is she still alive?"

"Just about," said Grimes. "No idea if the vet can save her."

"Dear Lord, how could anyone do such a thing?"

O'Ryan stood over him, beady eyes taking in everything. "Greed. Probably a burglary that went badly wrong, when the intruder was disturbed."

They were interrupted by the sound of someone else ringing the doorbell. Ian went to answer it, but Grimes indicated he'd see to it. He was gone only a few seconds, before he called for his superior to join him. Ian followed, feeling like he was trapped in a nightmare. A uniformed police officer was on his doorstep. The three of them talked quietly before O'Ryan and Grimes came back in.

"Well," said O'Ryan. "Looks like we can fix an exact time to when the incident occurred next door, Mr. Logan. Our experts estimate the old gent has been dead about sixteen hours, but we can be even more precise. Seems he raised his arm to try and protect himself, and his wristwatch got smashed in the attack. It stopped at five past one."

The thought of poor old Benjamin trying to fend off some murdering, thieving bastard made him feel sick.

O'Ryan's eyes narrowed. "Where were you in the early hours of this morning, Mr Logan?"

An odd buzzing sound erupted in his ears. He stood open mouthed. Then, with a gasp, he uttered, "You think I killed Benjamin Stanton?"

"Did you?" O'Ryan asked calmly.

"No, I bloody well did not. Why the hell are you accusing me? I liked the old chap. What the hell is this?"

"Enquiries, sir. Just routine enquiries."

Grimes had his notebook open again. "So, where were you last night between say eleven pm and two am?"

His heart was thudding. Beads of cold sweat were bursting out of his skin. He wanted to tell this pair to go fuck themselves, but the more he antagonised them the longer this would go on. "I worked late. Then, I visited a friend. I got home about two o'clock."

"And this friend will verify your movements, will he?"

"She," Ian corrected him, lowering his head. "And no, I doubt she'd do that, seeing as she's denied ringing me."

Without looking up, he felt the two officers summing up the situation, jumping to conclusions. It felt like a noose was tightening around his neck.

"If you could tell us Shelley de Main's address," suggested Grimes, his pencil poised.

Ian shook his head. "I can't. She's married. It would wreck her life if her husband found out."

Again, another silence. Then, Grimes said, "We can check your story with the utmost discretion, her husband need never know. So, her address, if you wouldn't mind. Just to save time."

Ian told them, hating himself for having to. He gulped down another mouthful of whisky. Shelley would think he was waging war against her. *God, as if he hadn't done enough to the poor woman.*

"And your wife, sir," asked Grimes. "If you could verify your wife's movements around that time."

"I've no idea what she was doing, leaving me, presumably." He slammed his glass down on the coffee table again, his face hot and flushed. "Look, you've got a murder out there to solve. Why the hell don't you get on with it, and leave my domestic problems to me?"

O'Ryan ignored his outburst. "So, she only left the marital home last night?"

"Yes!" Ian blurted out. "I discovered she'd gone when I got home, if you must know."

"And you've no idea where she's gone?"

Ian shook his head. "I wish to God I *did* know. It's been driving me crazy all day. I've rang her sister and her friends. No one's seen her."

"Does she have her own transport, Mr Logan?"

"Yes, a Mini. A yellow one."

"Registration number?"

Ian told them, and Grimes jotted it down. "We'll put this out for you, Mr. Logan. You'll soon have her home again."

"You do want her back, don't you, Mr. Logan?" O'Ryan asked, watching his reaction.

Ian's eyes fluttered shut in an effort to hold back the sudden tears. "Yes, Inspector. I want her back. I love them so much, this is killing me."

"Them?"

"She took my daughter with her, too."

O'Ryan spoke, his face expressionless. "So, your wife left here with your daughter possibly around about the same time as your neighbour was being burgled and murdered."

Ian stared from one to the other, a nauseous sensation rising inside of him. Surely there was no connection. Julia could have left him at any time during the day, straight after breakfast, for all he knew. But, when he spoke, it was to confirm the worse scenario. "Yes. Yes, it's possible."

Grimes got on his radio; he was reporting the Mini's registration number to someone, as he and O'Ryan strode out of the house.

Ian stood alone in the centre of the room, a cold dark despair crawling over him. Julia and Lucy might never be coming back.

Maybe they *couldn't* come back.

Chapter 19

Sweat glistened on Nash's pale skin, mingling with the drizzle. A cold mist hung in the air, as darkness fell. He'd had to work quick, well, quick for him, in the state he was in. He had no idea how long Vince would be gone. Knowing him, it would be his luck to find a car he could nick round the next bend. And this job had to be done before Vince got back. His life depended on it.

The dog bite had really taken it out of him. Normally, he'd be a match against Vince, if it came to a fight. However, now, he felt like he hadn't a scrap of energy left in his body.

It had been practically impossible digging and shovelling one-handed, and it was only thoughts of the consequences if this wasn't done right keeping him going. He had no strength left. His entire body ached now, especially his arm. It burned, and his face throbbed like he had a toothache.

He was a good distance from the house, in a rough overgrown copse, but he could still make out the chimneys, and boarded up top windows, silhouetted against the grey evening sky. He stared at the little attic window jutting out from the steep slate roof. The window wasn't covered, and he could almost imagine two faces up at the windowpane, peering out. Although, he knew they wouldn't. He'd told them to keep out of sight, and not make a sound. Maybe he was wrong to trust them. He should have finished them off, like Vince told him. Only, he didn't hurt kids. Kids dying broke your heart, he knew from experience. He didn't want to risk feeling like that ever again. And the woman had been kind to him. There weren't many people in this world who had showed him any kindness, but she had. Still, they'd better keep quiet, and out of sight. It wasn't just their lives at stake now.

All around was wild countryside. Skeletal trees, with their leafless branches, dripped cold spots of rain on his head, while beneath his feet, the ground was spongy with mud and fallen wet leaves.

He stood back, and wiped the sweat from his eyes with his good arm. The mound of soft earth was five and a half feet long by two feet wide. He'd dragged a few broken branches over it. It would have to do, he was knackered.

He flung the broken spade he'd been using into the undergrowth, and staggered back to the house. There was no warmth there. If anything, it felt colder and damper than outside. At least outside, the air smelt fresh, not rank with mould and decay. He lit the stove, and put his face close to the flame. The pain soared, and he groaned.

He wanted to sleep. He *needed* to sleep. At least when he was asleep, the pain eased. But, there was more to be done. Vince expected him to be ready when he returned with the vehicle. He wanted to be all ready, so they could go. But, everything had to be removed, so there was no sign of them ever being here.

He dragged himself upstairs to his bedroom. It was a desolate room, with an old mattress on the floor. He shoved the few bits of clothing he'd got into a bag, then went along to Vincent's room, and did the same there. Floorboards creaked and bowed, as he moved. Bloody death trap, this was. He had to drag the holdalls full of stolen stuff downstairs one at a time. He dumped it all in the kitchen, ready to go.

They'd travelled light, leaving most of their belongings behind in the flats they'd both walked away from. They'd both got their passports, though. There was no going back. Just moving on, starting again with the money they'd get from this job. He didn't care where Vince planned on heading. All he knew was he'd be booked onto a flight to sunny California by this time tomorrow.

He slumped down onto a chair, picturing himself, lying on a warm Californian beach, his face all fixed up, basking in the sunshine, listening to the ocean's waves lapping on a sandy shore, eyeing up the women, handsome again, picking and choosing. He could almost feel the warm sun on his face…

A rough shaking of his good arm jolted him awake. He blinked up to see Vince standing over him, surprised to find he'd fallen asleep.

"You done it?" Vince rasped.

"'Course I have," Nash answered, struggling to form the words. His jaw ached, like every other joint in his body.

"What've you done with them?"

"Buried them, out in the fields," said Nash, wiping his mouth. "Nearly killed me, dragging them all that way, but it's done. Did you get a car?"

"Naturally. A decent one. And I got us some chips. Want some?"

Nash tried to get to his feet. He couldn't manage it. He was probably weaker than he thought. He couldn't remember when he last ate. He wasn't hungry now, but the pains were back, crippling him. Food might help.

"Eat, then go?" he slurred.

"First thing in the morning," said Vincent, opening up the chip paper, and devouring the food ravenously.

Nash stared at him with bleak eyes. Tomorrow seemed a lifetime away. "Why not tonight? Let's get going. I gotta get out of this cold. It's killing me."

With his mouth stuffed with food, Vincent said, "No point. I can't see my friend in London until after eleven tomorrow. We may as well sleep here in some sort of comfort rather than risk being picked up roaming the streets or sleeping in a stolen car." He smiled. "You'll still be on a flight out to California by lunchtime. Eat up."

Nash unwrapped his bag of chips, but his movements were laboured, painfully slow. Vincent jabbed his mobile, tuning into the radio. He tapped his foot in time with the music, as he ate.

"So, you've cleaned up?" Vince asked, between mouthfuls.

"Yeah. There's nothing to see," Nash answered, his head lowered.

"Where did you say you buried them?"

Nash nodded towards the window, but the effort was almost too much, and he groaned. "Out there, among the brambles. Want me to show you?"

"You sure there's nothing left, no blood or anything? Think I'll nip upstairs and check."

"You calling me a liar?" Nash started to say, but Vince was already heading for the stairs. Nash paused between chewing, listening as the stairs creaked under his weight. He made no move. There was nothing for him to see up there, nothing to worry about. He'd even soaked the floor in water to make it look like he'd cleaned up blood.

When Vince returned, there was an odd look on his face. "You've done a thorough job, haven't you, my old mate? No one would ever have known they were here."

"Just done what you said," Nash muttered.

Vincent's eyes narrowed, and he peered towards the window. "So, they're out amongst the brambles, are they?"

"See for yourself. But, if you dig them up, you bury them again. I'm knackered."

Vince smiled. "Nice evening for a stroll."

"Please yourself," Nash murmured, but his stomach tightened into a knot, and he touched the cosh in his pocket. He staggered to his feet, and leaned in the open doorway. When Vince glanced back, he pointed vaguely to where he'd dug. Vince headed off into the shadows. Nash could make out his outline in the gloom of twilight. He saw him searching, then finally, stop, and stoop down.

Nash hadn't been listening to the music on Vince's mobile particularly, but then, the news came on, and the newsreader started saying something about an eighty-year-old antique dealer found battered to death at his home in Old church.

"Vince!" he shouted, drawing on some hidden energy to make his voice carry. "Vince, quick!"

The other man came leaping through the undergrowth. "What? What's happening?"

Nash jerked his thumb towards the mobile phone. Vince stood motionless, then quietly whispered, "That's us, matey. That's us."

Panic welled up inside Nash; he snatched at Vince's arm, pulling at the damp leather. "What we gonna do, Vince? They'll be after us now."

"Keep calm. Nothing's changed. They've got nothing to go on. And there was no mention of a woman and kid. They haven't linked them. Probably never will." He cast Nash one of his soothing smiles that usually made him feel better, not this time, though.

"We need to get out the area, head south."

Vince patted his shoulder. It felt more like a punch, in the state he was in. "Stop panicking. We'll go ahead with our little plan. Get ourselves a good night's sleep, and make an early start. My friend will take the stuff, pay us, and hang onto it, until everything has quietened down. And we'll be off to sunny climes, right?"

"Yeah, right, mate, sorry," Nash mumbled, feeling the panic subsiding slightly. "You want coffee?"

Vince cast him a long calculating look, making him fidget uneasily. He turned on the tap, holding the kettle beneath the running water, and avoiding Vince's eyes. Vince was brainy, much brainier than him—he wondered what he was thinking.

"You're a hard-hearted geezer," Vince said at last, sounding quite impressed.

Nash kept his mouth shut, and concentrated on trying to light the gas one handed.

Vince kept on staring. "You snuff out a woman and a kid, then you scoff a bag of chips, and ask if I want a coffee. You amaze me. Honest, Nash, you really amaze me."

A wave of relief washed over him. Deliberately, Nash tried to look irritated. "I didn't enjoy it, if that's what you're thinking. But, it was my side of the deal, you reckoned. Didn't have no choice, did I?"

"Indeed, you didn't," agreed Vince. "Because if I'd had to bloody my hands again, you wouldn't be entitled to one little bean, would you?"

The stove finally ignited, and Nash put the kettle over the flames. "Well, it's done. They're dead and buried. No one's gonna find them."

"How did you bury them? Couldn't have been easy one-handed."

Nash shuffled to a chair, and sat down again. He was tired, unbearably tired, and every limb ached. "It weren't easy. Go take a soddin' look, if you're that bothered."

"Keep your hair on, just taking a friendly interest," said Vince, spooning coffee into mugs. "They're dead and buried, so we haven't any worries, have we?"

Nash stared bleakly at the steaming mug of coffee Vince shoved under his nose a few minutes later. He had one worry—how to lift that mug up to his lips.

Chapter 20

Chief Inspector Patrick O'Ryan drained the last dregs of his vending machine coffee, squashed the plastic cup in his fist, and aimed it accurately at the bin on the other side of the office. Len Grimes raised his eyebrows in recognition of the good shot. It had been a hell of a long night, and their duty wasn't over yet.

O'Ryan had stayed at the crime scene until the early hours, establishing the method the perpetrator had used to get in, and the type of weapon used to kill the poor blighter. Whoever had attacked the old man had made certain he didn't live to tell the tale. It had been a particularly brutal attack. It was amazing to find he hadn't polished off the dog, too, out of spite, because there was human blood on its coat, so it had certainly tried to defend its owner.

O'Ryan had sent Len Grimes off to visit Shelley de Main during the evening. He returned later to tell him she'd reported being mugged the night before. A report and crime sheet had even been filed. When Len Grimes had called on her, she'd fobbed her husband off by saying it was more questions regarding her mugging. Len, being the nice guy, had gone along with it, until they'd been able to talk, without her husband listening. But, even then, she'd denied being with Ian Logan on the night of the crime, or phoning him.

It hadn't taken much detective work to trace the call Logan had received to find it had indeed been from her. So, chances were, he was telling the truth. At the adjacent desk, Len Grimes stretched his lanky frame. "What do you reckon then, sir? Think Logan's got anything to do with the old chap's death?"

O'Ryan swivelled in his chair. "Just pondering that same question, myself, Len. According to what Shelley de Main told you, she was at the cinema alone, and even managed to get herself mugged on the way home. So, that scuppered Logan's alibi."

"You don't think Logan walloped her then, sir?" Len Grimes suggested, tapping his pencil against his teeth. "She'd have to tell her old man something, wouldn't she? Mind you, she's a bit old for Ian Logan, a good ten years or more, I reckon."

O'Ryan sighed. "I see you still have a lot to learn, Len! There's more to life than young dolly birds. You'll probably find that out yourself, one of these days."

Len Grimes chuckled. "Wouldn't fancy her, myself. Too brassy. Might suit you though, boss."

O'Ryan pulled on a corduroy jacket, and then, his sheepskin. "I'm a happily married man. The question doesn't arise."

"Yeah, yeah," grinned Len Grimes, taking the lead from his superior, and getting his own coat on. "Where to, then, boss?"

"An early morning call, I think. We'll be doing him a favour. He might oversleep, with his wife away. And what I want to do is take a DNA swab. Forensics have detected two types of blood in the old man's hallway, and it's not Benjamin Stanton's on the dog. So, my guess is, the dog bit the bugger – and Logan has a couple of cuts on his hand and wrist, hasn't he?"

"Just small cuts though, boss, going by the size of his plasters. The amount of blood we found means the dog must have punctured a vein or an artery – a deep wound, anyway."

O'Ryan checked his car keys were in his pocket, and moved briskly. "Well, the sooner we eliminate him, the sooner we can expand our search."

Grimes followed smartly, buttoning up his coat against the biting cold wind, as they went out into the watery gloom of a November morning. "Shouldn't we get a warrant?"

"If he's got nothing to hide, we won't need one, will we?" said O'Ryan, ignoring the look his colleague cast him. He knew what he was thinking; he was like a dog with a bone. Only once he got an inkling about something, he didn't let go. And there was definitely some connection between Logan and this crime. What it was, he didn't yet know. But, he couldn't ignore his gut instincts.

"Not much to go on though, is there, sir?" Grimes remarked, sliding into the passenger side of the vehicle.

O'Ryan turned the ignition key, and put the wipers on. "You don't think so? Isn't it odd his wife shopped for the deceased, and vanished on the same night he was murdered?"

"So, you think Logan and his wife bumped the old guy off, then she nips off, with whatever they've nicked, so it's not found on their premises?"

"Stranger things have happened," said O'Ryan. "If she was a regular visitor to the old man, she would know what he had, and what was worth nicking. The neighbour on the other side has said the old man had a small fortune in antique silver and gold. I didn't see any evidence of it, so it looks like someone's nicked the lot."

"Well, unless he'd got it all logged with his insurance company, it's going to be a devil of a job knowing what has been stolen," remarked Grimes, buckling up, as O'Ryan pulled out of the police station.

The roads were pretty deserted at this hour of the morning, and happily, there was no fog. O'Ryan drove quickly and smoothly. "So, that's another good reason for tracking down Logan's wife. If she wasn't involved in this, then she might know what sort of stuff he had."

"I imagine the murder was a bit of a mistake," added Grimes, wiping the condensation from the side window. "The old chap probably caught them at it, and suffered the consequences. Although, they might have guessed the dog would have heard them though. Bit odd, that."

"The wife was a regular visitor to the house," O'Ryan reminded him. "The dog would have known her. Probably wouldn't have barked."

"Why hit it, then?" Then answering his own question added, "Though, I suppose, when they attacked the old man, the dog tried to defend him."

"Most likely," agreed O'Ryan. "However, like you pointed out, the attacker lost a lot of blood. You'd think it would need stitching. But, there's been no reports from casualty departments about anyone needing treatment for a dog bite."

He turned into the estate, leading to Sycamore Drive. They were nice houses around this part of the village. It was the sort of area he'd like to live in, if he had the money. But, you couldn't buy anything on a copper's wages around here. "We need to take a look at Logan's dirty washing, I'd say, Len."

"And his rubbish. See if there's a shirt with dog's teeth marks," said Grimes, adding, "I'm glad the dog is still hanging on in there. Lovely dog. She didn't deserve that."

"She certainly didn't, Len," agreed O'Ryan, as he pulled up outside Ian Logan's house. "But, neither did a harmless old man."

Chapter 21

Ian woke to a ringing in his ears. He rolled over, and felt the emptiness of the bed. His arm flopped heavily over his eyes. The ringing continued. *Phone? Doorbell?* He couldn't tell. He'd had too much whisky again last night. That would have to stop. He needed to keep his wits about him.

Struggling out of bed, he dragged on his dressing gown, and stumbled down the stairs.

Two figures were silhouetted through the slim panes of patterned glass in the door. They were too big to be his wife and daughter. He knew immediately who it was, and he heaved a sigh.

"Didn't wake you, did we, Mr. Logan?" the older detective remarked, not looking at all like he was sorry to have awoken him.

Talking to a sarcastic copper this time of day was the last thing Ian needed. "More questions, Chief Inspector O'Ryan? Or have you come to tell me you've done your job, and found the murdering swine who killed my neighbour, and we can all sleep easy in our beds again."

O'Ryan regarded him, with a small understanding smile. "We're making progress."

"Well, that's a surprise, considering I'm the only one you seem to be interrogating," Ian said, walking away from the door, knowing they wanted to come in. He went through to the kitchen, and filled the kettle.

"Not at work today, sir?" asked the other one, Grimes.

"No."

"Holiday?"

Ian looked acidly at them. "No."

"Sick leave, then?" O'Ryan suggested, glancing at the dressing on his arm.

"No. I'm taking the day off, in the hope of finding my wife and daughter."

"Where do you work, sir?" asked Grimes. His notepad was out again.

With a sigh, Ian told them, adding, "I'm making coffee, you want some?"

"That would be nice," said O'Ryan, following up with more questions about Ian's job. He wanted to know how long Ian had worked for his company, and if he was happy there—if he was in line for a promotion.

It was almost laughable. It was like they were looking for reasons now for him bumping his neighbour off. He handed them both mugs of coffee, and took a sip of his own. "At present, we don't have any money worries. I have a well-paid job, Inspector O'Ryan. I certainly don't need to go around stealing old men's valuables, if that's what you're getting at."

"I'm getting at nothing. Just trying to establish a picture of the people living in the vicinity of the deceased."

The officer nodded, added sugar to his coffee, then inspected Ian's hand. "How's the injuries this morning? Any better?"

"I don't know. I haven't looked. They feel okay."

"You want to keep an eye on them, sir," suggested Grimes. "You don't want gangrene setting in."

"Thank you for your concern. So, what exactly do you want to talk to me about today, or is it a social call?"

O'Ryan made himself comfortable on a kitchen chair, loosened his coat, and started playing idly with a silver teaspoon. "Benjamin Stanton, the deceased, how well did you know him?"

Ian sipped his black coffee. It cleared his head a little. "We've been neighbours about nine or ten years. He was here before that. We're on chatting terms."

"The neighbours seem to think he was a very wealthy man."

"He probably was," Ian conceded, with a shrug. "He's a retired antique dealer and collector – or rather, he was."

O'Ryan stirred his coffee. "Problem is, we've no idea what's been stolen. I imagine your wife would have a better idea, seeing as she's a regular visitor to his house. Have you any idea where she is, sir? We really do need to speak to her."

"And I don't?" Ian snapped, glaring at the senior officer.

Inspector Grimes had a more sympathetic tone to his voice. "Have you any idea what time she might have left home yesterday, sir?"

"I've told you. I got in around two a.m. I'd been out since early morning. She could have gone at any time."

"And did she take all her belongings with her?" Grimes asked.

Ian was about to snap out another indignant reply, when he realised he honestly didn't know what she'd taken. If she'd packed an overnight bag, it would imply she planned on coming back.

He didn't stop to explain, but bounded upstairs, and into the bedroom. Frantically, wondering why he hadn't checked this earlier, he threw open her wardrobe doors. His heart plummeted, as he saw her wardrobe was bereft of all her good clothes.

He stared at the empty coat hangers for some time, then crossed the room to the dressing table, and flipped open her jewellery box. Empty, practically, only the pieces she never wore — some earrings, a large silver and gemstone ring old Benjamin Stanton had given her last Christmas; nothing left of value, sentimental, or otherwise.

Ian sank down onto the bed, head in hands. No, she wasn't planning on hurrying home. She had left him—for good.

"This is silver, isn't it?" O'Ryan asked, startling him. He had come upstairs silently, and was now looking into Julia's jewellery box.

Furiously, Ian jumped up, and snatched the ring off him. "Who the hell gave you permission to come up here?"

O'Ryan looked steadily at him. Ian was a good six inches taller than the officer, but somehow, he had the knack of making him feel small and worthless. "We could always get a search warrant, Mr. Logan. It's entirely up to you."

Ian felt himself go weak at the knees. "A search warrant? What the hell are you accusing me of?"

"We're not accusing you of anything," said O'Ryan calmly. "But, that is antique silver, isn't it? I'm not an expert, but there are some things I recognise. Where did it come from?"

Ian felt as the noose growing tighter. He spoke with difficulty. "Benjamin Stanton gave it to my wife last Christmas, as a thank you for all she does for him. And if you don't believe me…"

"I can, what, sir? Ask the old man? I can't do that, because somebody smashed the poor soul's skull in, so they could get their greedy hands on shiny pieces of metal. Just like this one."

Chapter 22

Tiny particles of dust danced in the thin rays of light filtering through the grimy attic window. The pale watery beam fell on the two motionless figures, lying huddled together on a bed made of bin liners and old clothes, arms wrapped tightly around each other.

The warmth on Julia's cheek felt like someone's breath, and her eyes shot open, the fitful night's sleep gone, but the nightmare remaining.

Lucy slept on, as Julia's body tensed, ready to defend them – or attack, expecting someone to be standing over them. She half-expected to smell the leather of his coat, see his 'oh so handsome' face, smiling down on them. Or the scarred figure of the man sent to murder her and Lucy, and who, for some unknown reason, had switched from executioner to saviour. For a second, she feared he had changed his mind and returned to finish them off. But, there was no one there; no one standing over them with a club or a knife. It was a tiny ray of sunlight, touching her cheek.

Julia had thought Nash incapable of compassion or mercy. She had thought him to be a vile, pathetic, inhuman creation. Yet, he had surprised her, and she had found herself trusting him to the point of promising she and Lucy would stay up here in the attic, hidden and totally silent for twenty-hour hours, after hearing them leave. Only, they hadn't left—not yet.

Yesterday evening, after they'd spent hours playing dead under the blanket, Nash had returned. He'd told them to move quickly, no arguments. They were to get into the attic, and stay there, until he and the other one were long gone. Getting into the attic had meant climbing precariously on a rickety chair on top of a crate, and squeezing through a tiny, grimy trapdoor in the ceiling.

Lucy had sobbed quietly, as Julia had lifted her into the pitch-black void first. Then, the child had knelt by the opening, and helped Julia clamber in, her tears falling onto Julia's face.

"Not a sound, understand?" Nash had uttered. "I'm gonna tell him I've buried you. If he finds out you're still alive, we're all dead."

"Just let us go," Julia had pleaded. But, his compassion hadn't stretched that far, so she had nodded numbly, and slid the attic door hatch back into place herself, sealing them into their tomb.

The attic stank of mildew, and a freezing wind whistled through the eaves, with the force of a gale. Almost immediately, Julia had banged her head on a slanting timber beam, as she'd tried to stand. Then, she'd had to bend almost double, feeling her way along the rafters, fingers groping through thick cobwebs, clutching Lucy, terrified in case their feet slipped off the beams, and went through the plaster ceiling.

The blackness had been total, and Lucy had clung to Julia, trying not to sob out loud. She had held her, trying not to scream herself. Slowly, the hysteria had subsided, but they had both wept. Then, afraid Vincent would come back and hear them, she begged Lucy to be silent, and cradled her in her arms, until finally the child fell asleep.

She'd made her daughter as comfortable as possible. Plastic bin liners, full of old clothes, made for a bed across the beams. When Lucy was settled, Julia had battled her own panic, and forced herself not to give in to it. Instead, she felt around the room, crawling on all fours along the rafters, acclimatising herself to the darkness, and overcoming the suffocating claustrophobic sensation threatening her sanity.

It came as a surprise, as she felt the damp walls, that there was a small window. It was thick with grime. She spat on a rag, and rubbed vigorously, until she could see out. The palest grey light infiltrated the darkness, banishing the black void, helping her make sense of her surroundings.

For a long while, Julia had stood, gazing out, wondering if Ian was missing her – or was he with his mistress, enjoying the freedom. *Did he care that she was out of his life? Was he worried about them? Was he even aware of their predicament?* She doubted it.

For one despairing moment, Julia felt it really didn't matter if she died. It was a desolate, bleak thought – a dreadful hopeless emptiness. It was a feeling she had never experienced before – and never wanted to again. Then, through the shadows, she spotted Lucy, her small frame curled up on top of the pile of rubbish, and guilt for her selfishness overwhelmed her. The child was only eight; she had her whole life ahead of her. She *had* to get her out of this situation, somehow.

Anger towards the two individuals flowed fiercely through her veins, along with a burning desire to survive this, for Lucy's sake, if not her own.

All they had to do was remain quiet, until those two downstairs had left.

She had looked around for protection of some sort, and saw a wooden box. She was glad of its weight, as she dragged it, carefully and quietly, across the beams over the trapdoor At least with that there, no one could creep in, if she slept. Next, she sought out a weapon, deciding on an old chair leg. She wangled it back and forth breaking it off. It splintered easily, and she held it in both hands, swinging it through the air.

Now, she felt better, less vulnerable.

All they had to do was wait in silence, careful not to give their presence away to Vincent.

Julia heard him return, five or six hours after being secreted into the attic. She heard him on the stairs, talking to Nash, going in and out of bedrooms, looking for them. *Hadn't he believed Nash's story they were dead and buried?* He must eventually have believed Nash had disposed of their bodies outside, in a shallow grave, somewhere – because he didn't look in the attic.

The two men didn't leave, however, as Nash had said they would. She heard them go to bed, and she was certain they were still here.

Now, with the morning light struggling through the grimy window, Julia stretched her legs slowly, trying not to wake Lucy. Her ribs ached; her eye was puffed, almost closed. Everything hurt, her stomach rumbled, but at least Nash had had the humanity to leave them with a bottle of water.

It had been an eternity since she had eaten. Lucy had eaten most of her egg yesterday morning, but the child had to be starving, even though she hadn't complained.

Her thoughts drifted, imagining them sitting down with Ian for breakfast. She pictured him sitting across the table to her, his dark golden hair still ruffled from sleep, a little stubble around his strong jaw, blue eyes – as blue as Lucy's, looking at her, crinkling as he smiled. She imagined crispy bacon, fat sausages, and hot, sweet tea. She thought of walking hand-in-hand with Lucy to school, bringing her home again, and being in Ian's arms…

"Mummy!"

Her bubble burst, and her hand instantly covered Lucy's mouth, finger to her lips, but already afraid the cry would have sounded through the silent house. The child's eyes were huge, and Julia's heart ached, as she saw the fear returning to cloud her daughter's sweet, innocent face.

"Quietly, darling," Julia whispered, her hand still over Lucy's mouth. "We have to talk in tiny whispers, until they've gone. Be brave a little longer, please."

Lucy nodded, her eyes still like saucers. Julia took away her hand, smoothing the soft hair back from her daughter's troubled eyes. She held her close. "It won't be long now, I know it."

"I've got tummy ache. It hurts. It really hurts."

"You need the toilet?" Julia murmured, rubbing her daughter's tummy. "I know, me too."

Locked in the room downstairs, they had been allowed to use the toilet. For nearly twelve hours now, neither of them had gone.

"It really hurts," Lucy groaned, almost crying now.

"Hold on," Julia whispered, getting to her feet, finding that every muscle in her body screamed out in pain. "I'll organise us a loo." A quick look round had her deciding the far corner of the attic would suffice.

"Hold my hand, sweetheart, and be careful only to stand on the beams. The floor might not be strong enough to support us."

They carefully made their way to the far corner of the room, where some old newspapers were about to find a new role in life.

Each step was taken with utmost precision, making sure nothing creaked or cracked. Nothing must happen now to alert Vincent. She knew in her heart he wouldn't think twice about killing her and Lucy, if he had to. Nash, too, probably.

"I feel horrible," Lucy complained, as they relived themselves on the old newspapers.

"It can't be helped, love. Besides, no one lives here," Julia whispered back.

Stepping away from the makeshift toilet, Julia peeped out through the little window. It was obvious this was an attic window positioned in the roof, because she could see the steeply sloping roof below them. They were such a long way up, four stories high. It was an amazing and terrifying view; she could see for miles. There was farmland and forest, a church spire in the distance. She tried to get her bearings, wracked her brains to think where this four-storey derelict house could be. Surely, she would have driven past this at some time, or other.

Way down, in the drive – or what had once been a drive, before becoming overgrown with brambles, was another car parked beside her Mini. For a second, her hopes soared. *Had someone come to rescue them? The police?* No, she knew what it was. They'd stolen another car, one that worked. She prayed they would make their getaway soon.

Her eyes drifted off into the distance again. Beyond the treetops was farmland. She could see a farmhouse, and sheep grazing in the fields.

It all appeared so peaceful, so calm. Her thoughts drifted to those long lazy days when she, Lucy, and Ian would go walking in the countryside. They had their favourite places. This time of year, they loved walking through the woods, eyes peeled for squirrels, taking a few branches of red-berried holly to decorate the mantelpiece at Christmas. They would walk along the canal tow-path, with its ducks and moor hens, and Lucy would run on ahead through the tunnel, shouting back at them, so she could hear her voice echo. It seemed like a lifetime ago, when life was good.

She rested her forehead against the windowpane, unable to stop the sudden rush of tears. She was trying hard not to sob out loud, and to be strong, for Lucy's sake. It would be over soon. Those two downstairs would leave before long, and she and Lucy would be free.

"Mummy, what's wrong?"

"Nothing, I'm alright," Julia murmured, wiping her eyes on her sleeve.

Lucy was up on her feet, "Are you frightened? Are they going to come back and hurt us?"

"Of course not," Julia said softly, as Lucy came towards her. "Be careful love, watch where you're stepping…"

Before Julia could reach out to her daughter, Lucy's foot slipped off the beam. There was a sickening crack of plaster, as the child's foot broke through the floor.

Her scream was out, before Julia could stop her.

Chapter 23

Vincent's eyes shot open. His heart was banging inside his chest. The kid. That had been the kid's scream, unless it was a bird, or some creature outside being ripped apart by a fox. Or it was a dream. But, it might have been the kid, still alive.

He lay perfectly still, listening. The house was silent now, like it was holding its breath. He couldn't take the risk. He pulled on his trousers and shoes. It *had* been a scream; he wasn't one to imagine things. It had come from somewhere above – the top of the house. Cursing to himself, he realised he hadn't searched everywhere last night. The kid was alive. *What about the woman?* Her, too, probably.

Teeth gritted he stormed out of his room, slamming his foot against Nash's bedroom door, sending it crashing back against the wall, making enough noise to wake the dead.

Nash lay sprawled on his mattress, shivering. His skin was the colour of cold porridge. Vincent grabbed him by his denim jacket, and dragged the shaking skinny little runt to his knees. His eyes half opened, bleak hopeless eyes.

"You didn't do it, did you?" He shook him, finding no resistance. It was like shaking a rag doll, and all the hate and resentment for putting up with his ugly mush all this time consumed him.

Vincent hit him hard across his scarred face, with the back of his hand. Spittle sprayed out of Nash's mouth. "Why didn't you? Huh? Why?"

Saliva continued to dribble from the corner of Nash's mouth. His words were vague, barely audible. "They're dead… told you… buried…"

Vincent's face contorted with fury. "They'd better be, or you're gonna be buried out there, dead or alive." He slammed him viciously onto his back, and stormed out of the room.

The stairs swayed, as he ran down them, and, for a second, he stopped, and clutched at the wall, thinking they were about to go. They groaned, but stayed put. He took the last stairs more cautiously. Outside, it was bitterly cold despite a winter sun. He broke into a run, leaping the brambles, cursing as his coat caught and snagged.

He searched around, trying to work out where he'd seen the mound of earth last night. He could hardly believe his own stupidity for actually believing the little runt. He should have known. He should never have trusted him.

It wasn't difficult to find the grave again. The betraying little bastard may as well have marked it with a cross and flowers.

Working feverishly, he began tearing the sticks and bracken aside, finding soft loose earth below. Without a shovel, he used his hands, scooping out handfuls of mud and worms. Then, he felt something – material, a damp woollen blanket. His stomach churned, doubts crowding him. Nash could have done them in after all.

Then, what was the scream? He didn't believe in ghosts. It had been the kid; he was positive. He'd heard enough of her high-pitched shrieks to last a lifetime. But, now, he felt uncomfortable as his fingertips touched the blanket that the kid had been wrapped in. He didn't want to see their mangled corpses. But he had to be sure. He pulled at it, and felt the weight of something wrapped inside it. He tugged harder. Stones and mud came tumbling out.

Throwing back his head, Vincent roared with blinding rage. And then, with his fury taking over, he stumbled back to the house, murder in his heart. He ran up the stairs three at a time, ignoring the sounds of cracking wood.

Nash was struggling to get off the mattress when Vincent lunged at him, fists and feet flaying, finding their target with brutal accuracy. Nash curled himself into a ball, his good arm trying to fend off the crippling blows.

"Why? Why didn't you finish them off? Why?"

Cowering, Nash mumbled, "Don't kill kids. Not little kids."

"You do, when they're witnesses," Vincent snarled, landing another kick into the small of Nash's spine.

"Not kids," Nash uttered, as Vincent stood over him, waiting for an explanation. "Had a brother once, baby brother."

Vincent threw back his head in disgust. "Spare me the hearts and flowers."

Nash's bloodied face looked pathetically up at him. "Nobody gave a damn about me, except him. He loved me. He was two, I was thirteen. Giving him a bath, weren't I. Someone knocked the door, so I went downstairs for a minute… only a minute. Came back, and he was dead. Drowned." His drooped eyes met Vincent's. "You don't kill little kids. Never want to see another dead kid again, as long as I live."

"Well, that ain't going to be for much longer," Vincent growled. "And the woman? Don't tell me, you used to have a mother…"

"She was kind," Nash slurred. "Only two people have looked at me without wanting to puke, since me face got sliced up – you and her."

"You stupid, dumb idiot! She cares about you as much as I do. And you know how much that is? Zilch! Zero. Truth is, Nash, you turn my stomach. You always have. Only I put up with you, because I thought you would be useful to have around. But, you're not. You're an ugly waste of space. So, I'm gonna do your job for you, and I'm gonna hand the corpses to you when I've done, kid and all."

"Vince, no!" Nash whined, struggling to get to his feet, as Vincent strode out into the hallway. "They won't tell…"

Ignoring him, Vincent went up to the third floor, taking his time, opening doors, and searching properly, looking in cupboards, under piles of junk. Anywhere they might be hiding.

There was no sign in any of the upstairs rooms. He stood for a moment, looking up at the tiny attic trapdoor in the ceiling. *Could they have squeezed up there?*

If they were desperate enough, he realised.

He fetched a chair from a bedroom, his fury abating. A sadistic hatred for them all now running through his veins.

Standing on the chair, stretching up he could reach the trapdoor. He pushed upwards. It lifted a fraction, but there was a weight over it – something heavy, possibly even the woman sitting on it.

He was going to need something else to stand on so he could get his shoulder to it. He searched around. In the front bedroom, there was a wooden storage crate. Turned on its side, with the chair on top, he'd be able to reach. But, scrutinising the ceiling further along, he spotted something else. A hole.

A cold, calculating smile spread across his face. Walking back to stand directly under the trapdoor on the landing, he began to sing. "*Come out, come out wherever you are.*"

He listened. He could almost hear their terrified breathing. He could imagine them clinging on to each other, trying not to make a sound. He stood on the chair again, and pressed upwards. Again, the trapdoor gave a little, before it was snapped hard down. They were pressing down on it.

He liked this game. It made him want to sing again. "*Come out, come out wherever you are. Vincent's coming to get you…*"

Chapter 24

Nash couldn't tell what hurt the most, his body from the dog bite and the kicking, or knowing Vince had been pretending all this time, and he was as repulsed by the sight of him as the rest of the human race. He'd put on an act, making out he wasn't sickened by his appearance, and pretending they were mates. And all that time, it had been a big fat lie. He concluded both hurt equally—the deceit and the beating.

Well, Vince Webb was gonna be sorry. The smarmy bastard was forgetting who he was dealing with. Nash rolled onto his knees, reached for his cosh lying on the floor where he'd left it last night as he'd tried to sleep. It felt heavier than usual – unless he was getting weaker. He slipped it back inside his jacket, into the deep pocket he'd adapted years ago, next to the Stanley knife. It weighed him down, as he hauled himself to his feet.

His legs were like lead weights, not wanting to budge. But he had to move, he had to. He dragged himself to the door; sweat pouring out of him. He could hear Vince up on the next landing, singing. Well, he wouldn't be singing for much longer. But, before he saw to him, there was something else that needed seeing to. He reached the stairs, but instead of going up a flight to where Vince was, Nash crept downstairs, barely making a sound. It wouldn't take a minute – what he had to do. He felt for his Stanley knife, and staggered outside.

He was close to exhaustion, when he returned a few minutes later. He hoped Vince hadn't reached the woman and kid yet. They were decent—they were. Bloody shame they'd got tangled up in all this. They didn't deserve it.

He needed to get up those stairs. There was still time; he could hear Vince still singing, goading them, frightening the shit out of them.

Drawing the cosh out of his jacket, he climbed the stairs, but it was too heavy to carry in one hand. He was weakening. Vaguely, he wondered if he was dying, like the woman had warned all along. His hatred for Vince deepened. He must have seen it coming, and he hadn't given a shit.

He put the cosh back inside his jacket, and concentrated on lifting one foot after the other. The stairs groaned under his weight, but the sound and movement didn't cause Vince to come searching; he was too intent on his manic chanting.

Looking upwards through blurred eyes, the stairs seemed to reach upwards forever, like a mountain, stretching to some far-off point. Hatred forced him on. Vince Webb was gonna pay. If it took every last ounce of strength, he'd make the lying bastard wish he'd never set eyes on him.

He struggled on, half on his knees, crawling, holding back the grunts of pain. He had to be quiet. But, each stair took its toll, until he couldn't tell whether it was his head swaying and rolling, or the staircase about to give way and collapse.

Nearing the top of the second flight, Nash raised his eyes to see Vince had his back to him. He was standing on a chair, underneath a hole in the ceiling, singing his stupid song. Reaching the top stair, Nash hauled himself from his belly to his feet, and gripped the cosh. He took two unsteady steps towards the man he had stupidly thought was his friend, hoisted the weapon, and then, brought it slamming down onto the back of Vince's knees. With a shriek of agony, he buckled instantly, and fell sprawling across the landing, moaning in pain, chair legs tangling with limbs.

Nash slumped back against the wall, breathing hard, trying to find some reserves of strength. You didn't leave a wild animal wounded, so it could come back and kill you. You moved in first.

He lunged again, metal bar raised, but Vince kicked out, knocking Nash's feet from under him. Vince was on him in a moment, punching and gouging. Nash fought back, lashing out wildly with his cosh, but his aim missed its target every time, and each blow took its toll on Nash's energies. They rolled towards the top of the stairs, then, Vince was standing, his face twisted with rage. Nash had always thought Vince was a great looking bloke. He had envied his appearance, however, now, he looked as ugly as he did, and Nash envied nothing.

Nash was dragged to his feet, and then, Vince struck him a vicious punch to his throat. He felt his airway seal, felt his lungs scream out for oxygen, felt his eyes bulge. As he gasped for breath, his head was yanked backwards, until he was looking into Vince's blotched and ragged face.

With no breath to draw on, Nash felt himself falling backwards. Everything was spinning, there was a gurgling sound coming from somewhere close by. Maybe it was him, he couldn't tell. Then, noise was all around him—a cracking, splintering, groaning sound. The sound of the staircase, as it finally parted with the wall.

Shock registered on Vince's face, as he jerked backwards.

Nash reached out, desperately clawing at thin air, as the stairs fell away. The sensation was strange, like he was floating. Vince was getting further away – up above him now. He was floating in slow motion; he could see every trace of astonishment on Vince's face, as he floated so very slowly away from him.

There was time to think. He hoped the kid would be okay, and the woman. She'd plucked glass splinters from his brow. She'd said sorry when he'd yelped. He hoped they'd be alright, but he didn't think they would be, not now. Then, that thought faded, as the distance between him and Vince increased. He could see an aeroplane, waiting to take him to the Californian sunshine. It began taxiing along the runway, and he wanted to shout, tell it to wait.

But, as the floor rushed up to crush the final breath from his lungs, he saw the plane climbing into the blue sky, leaving him lying there to die among the rubble.

Chapter 25

Beads of perspiration glistened on Ian Logan's top lip. This was insane. He hadn't done old Benjamin in. *Why the hell would he?* He liked the old fella, but trying to get through to these thick coppers was like beating your head against a brick wall. They wouldn't listen; they'd made up their minds. God almighty, O'Ryan had even asked if he could take a DNA sample. "Just to eliminate you from our enquiries," he'd said, with that arrogant look on his face.

Of course he'd agreed. *How could he refuse?* But, this was all getting ridiculous. He was their scapegoat. It would make their job nice and easy, if they pinned the blame on him.

He dressed slowly, having persuaded them to at least allow him to get some clothes on. They were downstairs, nosing about, no doubt, and seeing what else they could pin on him.

Buttoning his shirt, and pulling on a sweater, he crossed to the window, and saw the hordes of police in the street, some milling around old Benjamin's garden. The house was all taped off, along with half the street. *Poor old devil*, Ian thought to himself. *Who the hell had done it, and half-killed the dog to boot?* There were some callous bastards about.

He spotted a uniformed police officer heading towards his front door. Cursing softly, he went downstairs to see what this one wanted.

"Could I have a word with the Chief Inspector, please, sir?"

"Wait there. I'll get him," Ian answered, not about to have another copper in his house. Two was more than enough. "Inspector O'Ryan, you're wanted outside," he said, going into the lounge, where sure enough they were looking through his sideboard drawers. "And from now on, I don't want you touching anything, unless you have a search warrant. And that's not because I'm hiding anything; it's because I object to police harassment."

O'Ryan did no more than raise one eyebrow, as he walked past him to the front door. Ian glared after him, running his fingers raggedly through his hair. The two officers talked quietly on the doorstep. He couldn't make out what they were saying. He hoped to God they weren't concocting something else to try and blame him for. He turned his back on them, and went through to the kitchen. Coppers, or no coppers, he was going to have some breakfast.

Fat splattered, as he threw two rashers of bacon into a pan. His kitchen was a mess; Julia was going to have a fit when she came home. The hollow feeling in his chest worsened – *if* she came home.

Grimes stood in the doorway, with a hungry look on his face. Ian tried to ignore it, and failed.

"You accuse me of murder, then you want me to cook breakfast for you?"

"Been on duty all night, sir. My stomach thinks my throat's cut."

Without a word, Ian threw a couple more rashers in.

"Actually, though, sir," said Grimes, leaning against a cabinet. "No one has accused you of anything. We're trying to piece it all together."

"But, you're barking up the wrong tree. Can't you understand that? What's going on here is a domestic problem. I've been a bloody fool, and my wife's left me because of it. It's got absolutely nothing to do with what's happened to my neighbour."

"Unfortunately, Mr. Logan," said O'Ryan, coming back into the kitchen. "I think you could be mistaken there."

Ian swung round, wanting to punch some sense into the thick copper, sick and tired of these accusations. However, instead of his usual, smug look, the officer's face carried an element of pity.

"What?" Ian demanded, feeling uneasy suddenly, as if they'd found some incriminating evidence proving he was guilty. An irrational thought leapt into his head, maybe he *was* guilty—had done old Benjamin in, and blocked it from his mind. Or, Julia had robbed the old man.

This was sending him insane. No wonder people admit to crimes they didn't commit under pressure.

O'Ryan was taking an infuriating long time to answer, as if selecting his words with the utmost care. "Your wife would have been driving a yellow Mini, you say, sir?"

Ian nodded, the smell of sizzling bacon suddenly losing its appeal.

O'Ryan continued staring at him, with that sympathetic expression on his face. It was disconcerting.

Ian's brow furrowed, as he saw O'Ryan cast a look in Grime's direction. The younger officer seemed to grasp some unspoken message. "For God's sake, will you tell me what's happening."

The Chief Inspector took a step closer. "Going by the time you returned home, on the night in question, and found your wife and daughter gone, it's feasible she could have left the house sometime between twelve-thirty and two a.m."

"She could have left at any time during the day," Ian replied, but guessing – hoping she would have given him the benefit of one last chance, to see if he came home at the appointed hour. And then, he remembered that Lucy's bed had been slept in. So, Julia had taken her from her bed when she'd made her decision to leave, realising he wasn't coming home at his usual time. He lowered his head. "Yes, it's feasible – probable, I suppose. They would have left around then." As soon as he'd spoken, he felt a tightness in his throat. The police had pinpointed Benjamin's attack to five past one in the morning. *Was this another link pointing the finger at him and Julia?* "So, what are you getting at?"

O'Ryan closed the space between them, and put a hand on Ian's shoulder. He half expected him to say, 'you're nicked, mate,' but then, Ian saw the sympathy behind his eyes, and realised it was a gesture of comfort.

"What?" he repeated, realising his voice this time was barely a whisper.

"My officers have found evidence in the road of a collision. They've found broken indicator glass and flakes of paint. Dark blue… and yellow."

He'd seen that himself, hadn't he? Broken glass in the road. It didn't mean anything. He certainly hadn't connected it to Julia's car. A sick feeling rose in his throat. *Why the devil hadn't he connected it? Was he stupid?* Had he been so wrapped up in his own self-pity he hadn't thought what Julia might have gone though.

"But, it was a bit of glass, just a bump." His frown deepened. They were still looking at him with solicitous expressions on their faces, as if waiting for him to fathom something out. And then, his legs felt weak. He stepped away from O'Ryan, and sank down onto the sofa, trying to make sense of this latest bit of news. She'd collided with another car. And who else might be out driving around these quiet streets in the middle of the night. Unless it was the person who'd attacked Benjamin… "Oh God!"

O'Ryan's sat down beside him. "Mr. Logan, we have to consider the worst. It's possible that your wife was leaving here, probably in a bit of a state, just as Benjamin Stanton's killer was leaving the scene of the crime, also in a bit of a state, judging by the amount of blood he'd lost."

Ian stared at him, his thoughts too jumbled to sort into any kind of logical sequence. "What are you telling me?"

"We discovered two blood types at the scene," explained O'Ryan. "One belonged to the victim. The other hasn't been identified as yet, which was why we wanted a DNA swab from you."

Giving his DNA was the last thing on his mind now, as the reality hit him. His wife and child could have come into contact with a murderer. More than that, crashed cars, and that would lead to what…

"God!" he breathed. "Oh, dear God!"

Grimes spoke up. "Even if the flakes of paint do come from your wife's car and the attacker's car, my guess is he wouldn't have stopped to exchange names and insurance details. He'd want to be well away."

It didn't make Ian feel any better. He knew Julia. If she'd had a bump in her car, she would stop, get out, see if anyone was hurt. "My wife wouldn't have driven away. She would have checked no one was injured."

"But, the offender wouldn't have hung around," said O'Ryan. "He wouldn't want to draw attention to himself."

"It would be a bit late for that," said Ian, getting to his feet, a cold panicky sweat starting to trickle down his neck. "Julia would have seen him, seen the car. My daughter would have seen him." His voice dried in his throat, as an awful scenario began to materialise in his head.

"We can't jump to conclusions, but we also have to assume the worst."

"They've been taken hostage! That's why they didn't turn up at her sister's. That's why Lucy's not at school. It's why no one has seen them."

"I doubt that very much," O'Ryan said, exchanging glances with his colleague, on his feet, too, now, urgency in his movement. "No point in jumping to conclusions. No perpetrator in his right mind would hardly want the complication of two hostages."

"But, he's not in his right mind," Ian shouted, pacing the room, needing to do something, and desperately needing his wife and daughter here now, safe with him. He turned to O'Ryan, frantic. "He'd just killed a helpless old man. He's not going to drive off, and leave them to call the police. Because you would, wouldn't you. If someone crashed into you, and then drove off, you'd call you cops. He'd know that. He wouldn't let them do that. He'd stop them identifying him, one way or another."

"Try and keep calm, Mr. Logan," Grimes said, getting on his radio. "The assailant wouldn't have been able to drive your wife's car *and* his own, so abduction isn't a likelihood. Wherever she went after the bump, she's gone of her own free will."

Ian tried to calm down. Grimes had a point there. "Yes, I suppose you're right. One man can't drive two vehicles…" His voice trailed away, as the same thought seemed to strike all of them. He saw it in O'Ryan's face, and in the younger officer's expression. But, Ian was the one to put it into words. "What if there was more than one…"

O'Ryan jerked his head, indicating Grimes to move. The taller officer strode out into the hall; he was already on his radio. Ian distinctly heard the words, 'hostage situation,' before his front door shut.

Blind panic made his head spin. He slammed his fists against the wall. "All this time you've wasted questioning me. They could be anywhere. What's happened to my wife and my little girl? She's only eight. Oh, my God, if they've hurt her…"

"No point in letting imagination get the better of you, sir," said O'Ryan. "Now, if you have a recent photograph of your wife and daughter, that will be a help. Then, if you wouldn't mind phoning family and friends – anyone who she might have gone to, just to see if they have turned up. And try and think if any of your neighbours owns a dark blue car. The bump hopefully has nothing to do with the crime."

Ian's head was beginning to throb. It was hard to think straight. "I don't know… a few of the neighbours have dark coloured cars – blue, grey, I don't know. You don't notice these things."

"Just try and keep calm, Mr. Logan. If we can keep a level head, we've more chance of finding your wife and daughter sooner, rather than later."

It was hard to put two coherent thoughts together. "It's bound to be those bastards' car. Sycamore Drive leads off into the countryside. We don't get passing traffic. People either live here, or they're visiting, or delivering something, or…"

"Let's not jump to conclusions, but if you could find those photographs, that would help."

He couldn't even think where any photos would be. They were all on his computer. Then, he remembered the ones in his wallet, and the framed one in the hall. He tried to get his panic under control.

"Calmly now, sir. More haste, less speed."

Ian glared at the police officer, despising him for wasting so much time when his wife and daughter's lives were in peril. "Why photos? How are photos going to help find my wife and daughter? They haven't run away, or are wandering lost somewhere."

"It helps us to know who we're looking for. Now, try and keep calm, sir. No point in getting too worked up."

Ian looked O'Ryan directly in the eye, and wondered whether he'd be collected, if it was his wife and child missing. In the calm manner, the police officer seemed to expect, Ian said, "Tell me something, Chief Inspector O'Ryan."

"Yes, sir?"

"If you had just smashed in an old man's skull, stolen all his possessions, then bumped into two people who could identify you, what would you do?"

O'Ryan didn't answer.

Chapter 26

Chief Inspector O'Ryan left the house, with Ian Logan's words ringing in his ears. He hoped to God the paint flakes weren't from the assailant's car. If he – or they—had taken Mrs. Logan and her daughter, he didn't hold out much hope for them. They'd be dead and dumped by now, poor buggers.

His arms swung briskly, as he walked down the drive, and out into the street. There was intense activity going on in the victim's garden, where more blood had been found. There was a trail of blood leading from the back of the house to the street, where it stopped, probably because the attacker had got into his getaway car. He hoped it was the perpetrator's blood, not the Logan woman's or her kid's. The trail could have been from the road to the victim's garden. Quite possibly it was Mrs. Logan's blood, or the little girl's.

This line of thought sent him barking out more orders for an even more in-depth search of the garden, specifically looking to see if a body had been buried there, or, to be more precise, two bodies.

Cold and weary, Grimes wandered over to him. It had been a long night. Although, if Mrs. Logan and her daughter were still alive, by some remote chance, no doubt their night had been a lot longer, and a damn sight more harrowing.

"With luck," said Grimes, "whoever killed the old man has taken the woman and kid along for insurance. Or, better still, their paths didn't even cross."

"You never know," agreed O'Ryan.

"Want me to pop back in, and ask him what his wife and daughter's blood groups are?"

"Do that, Len. Only try and be tactful. Tell Logan it's routine enquiries. Don't let on about all this blood."

"I'll get onto it."

"And see if there's any progress on matching the glass and paint flakes. If we can identify the other vehicle, then we've something to go on."

"It seems to indicate there was more than one perpetrator, wouldn't you say, sir?" Grimes suggested. "One person couldn't have driven two vehicles."

"He could have snatched the kid, and made Mrs. Logan follow," said O'Ryan, turning up his collar, a chill running through him his sheepskin jacket couldn't keep out. "Step on it, Len. Let's get things moving. I know chances are they're lying dead in a ditch somewhere, but if this is a kidnapping, and they're being held captive by some murdering swine, they're in one hell of a tight spot."

Chapter 27

Julia and Lucy lay sprawled across the wooden box they'd dragged over the trapdoor, pressing hard down, using their weight to hold the hatch shut. They clasped their hands tightly together, afraid to move, afraid to release the pressure on the trapdoor, even though the house was silent now.

They had shrunk back in horror, when Vincent had begun chanting. Lucy had wept in terror at the sound of his manic voice. They'd pressed desperately down on the trapdoor to stop him getting in.

Then, they had listened to the vicious fight that had gone on between the two men. Something dreadful had happened. They'd heard the horrendous sound of something falling away; a tremendous cracking sound, as if the house was collapsing. The entire house had shaken. She guessed it was the staircase, and because the fighting had stopped, she presumed one of them had probably perished. She hoped and prayed they'd *both* been killed, but she didn't dare raise the trapdoor yet to look, in case Vincent was still there.

Lucy's little face was covered in tear-streaked grime. Somehow, she'd managed to hang onto her teddy bear. But, both were afraid to speak out loud yet. Julia mouthed silently to Lucy, "I'm so sorry, my darling."

Lucy squeezed her hand, and mouthed back, "I love you, mummy."

"I love you, too, so very much."

After a few more minutes of silence, Lucy asked softly, "And you still love my daddy, don't you?"

Julia nodded. It was what Lucy needed to hear. But, deep down, there was no love in her heart for anyone except her daughter. If it hadn't been for Ian's infidelity, none of this would have ever happened.

She seriously wondered whether they would get out of this alive. *Would Ian realise what they'd gone through? Would it occur to him that they'd gone through hell these last few days? Was he even bothered, or was he consoling himself with his other woman?* She wondered who she was. Someone from work, no doubt. She'd met a few of them. There was only one who was brassy – who looked the sort to have an affair. She wondered if Ian loved her.

"Have the horrible men gone?" Lucy whispered.

"I don't know," she murmured. She wished she knew the answer. Either they had killed each other, or Vincent was on the other side of this trapdoor, toying with them, taking sadistic pleasure in this cat and mouse game.

Long agonising minutes passed, with them listening for any sound from below to indicate whether death lay waiting for them or freedom. From up in the eaves, a blackbird started to sing, and a shaft of dusty sunlight streaked through the attic window. It fell on their faces, warming them. Slowly, it moved, brightening in turn each murky corner of their prison.

Her body ached from lying in one position for so long, and her ribs still hurt from the beating Vincent had given her. She helped Lucy to sit up on the box, knees tucked under her chin. She did the same, keeping her weight pressed down, barely making a sound. Lucy's glistening eyes didn't waver from her face, as she was manoeuvred from one position to another, silently. Like Julia, Lucy knew the danger, and was doing her best not to do anything wrong. She cuddled close to Julia, and they sat, arms entwined around one another.

Eventually, a faint glimmer of hope began to rise inside of Julia. It had been so quiet below for such a long time now, she really began to wonder if both men had perished. Or they'd gone. If there was anyone lurking on the landing, surely, they would have heard some sound by now.

She had to know. They couldn't sit here forever. She had to try and see.

As gently as she could, she untangled herself from her daughter's arms, and slid off the box. She stood on the beams, heart pounding.

Lucy watched her, eyes widening in fear. Julia put a finger to her lips, and helped Lucy to stand safely. Every nerve in her body was tingling, every muscle taut and coiled, ready to throw her weight back over the box, if the trapdoor started to move. Nothing happened.

She looked at Lucy. Her blue eyes were like saucers. "I'm going to take a peep," she whispered. Then, moving the box a fraction of an inch at a time, Julia eased it off the trapdoor. The scratching of wood against wood was amplified to astronomic proportions. Time and again, she stopped to listen and look, her breath locked inside her chest.

There was still no sound from below, and Julia knelt down, and carefully lifted the trapdoor a fraction. She gasped at the carnage below. The stairs were gone; a gaping hole yawned where they had stood. She could see someone lying crumpled and motionless on the ground floor beneath a mass of timber. From this angle, she couldn't be sure who it was. She prayed it was Vincent.

A tiny thread of hope began to grow inside of her. Maybe they were safe, and this nightmare was over. "We'll try and get down, love," Julia murmured. "I'll lower myself down, you follow, and I'll be able to catch you."

Lucy was reluctant to let her go, and wrapped her arms around her fiercely. "Don't, Mummy..."

"We can do it, we can. But, you have to be very brave."

For a second, Lucy clung onto her mother's waist, afraid to let her go. Julia gently eased herself free, and felt for the weapon she'd spotted earlier—the chair leg – just in case. "Are you ready, sweetheart…"

It was at that moment she felt someone watching them. It was an instinct, yet so strong, she felt her skin crawl with terror.

She spun around, her gaze sweeping across the attic floor. She saw the vile apparition, and the scream building up within erupted, bouncing off the cobweb-blackened walls, and returning to ring in her ears. Lucy's scream was higher pitched—a sound no mother should ever hear.

Vincent was grinning up at them; his head and neck protruding through the plasterboard floor, where Lucy's foot had gone through earlier. It was a horrendous, disembodied face—watching, leering, delighting in their terror.

Julia's reactions were swift and automatic; pure gut response. She leapt from beam to beam, gripping her weapon – the chair leg. On reaching her goal, she let her arms fly, with a perfectly executed and powerful swing, bringing the chair leg swiftly down, like a golfer swinging his club. The rotten wood exploded into a million splintered fragments against the side of Vincent's head.

For a second, nothing happened. He didn't cry out, didn't curse. Even his smile remained intact. Julia stood trembling. *Had she missed? Had she hit the floor rather than his head? Was he now going to pull himself up through the floor, and murder them both?*

Mesmerised, she stared into his face, and then, his pale eyes rolled upwards into his head, until only the whites were visible. His mouth became slack, his expression vacant. Then, as if his legs had buckled, or whatever he was standing on had given way, he slid back down through the hole in the floor. The silence lasted a heartbeat, and then, came the crunch of wood and human flesh hitting the landing. "Mummy, have you killed him?" Lucy shrieked.

Julia peered down through the hole. He was lying tangled with an old box and a chair, the same ones she and Lucy had climbed on to get up here. But, he wasn't dead. He was writhing, clutching his head, blood oozing from between his fingers.

Sick with regret, she shook her head. "I should have, Lucy. I should have killed him, while I had the chance."

Chapter 28

The room was spinning and a kaleidoscope of coloured stars danced in front of Vincent Webb's dazed eyes. The pain was excruciating, blinding, and what angered him most was, it had been his own stupid fault. He hadn't expected her to attack. He'd thought she would be too freaked out to move. He'd expected her to back off, not come at him like a maniac. He'd underestimated her. But, she would pay. She would definitely pay, this time.

Rolling onto his back, he tried to focus on the hole in the ceiling. The spinning slowed down, and then, he saw her face peering down through the hole at him, like he was a freak in a sideshow.

He screamed out a string of obscenities, and staggered along the landing to the stairs – or what had been the staircase. He held onto the wall to keep his balance, and stared down at Nash's crumpled body below. The sight of him lying twisted, staring up with blank, sightless eyes, turned his stomach. He was as ugly dead as he was alive. He turned away, and began to formulate a plan.

Revenge for the smack on the head meant he had to get downstairs. He'd finish her off, good and proper. Kneeling, he checked the landing's floorboards, to make sure they wouldn't give way under his weight. They felt fairly sound, and so, hanging onto the edge of the landing boards, he eased himself over the stairwell, until he was hanging by his fingertips. Then, he began to swing, gauging where he wanted to land – away from Nash's dead body, and the worst of the smashed staircase. His head was pounding, and blood dripped into his eyes, as he swung back and forth. At the right moment, he let go.

Although he landed with knees bent to lessen the impact, it jarred his body, and another cascade of shooting stars danced before his eyes.

When he was steady enough to walk, he checked there was nothing left in the bedrooms that might indicate they'd ever been here, and went downstairs. He was glad they hadn't gone the same way as the top stairs, although, they were loose and swaying. It wouldn't take much to make them collapse, too.

He'd load the stolen stuff into the car in a bit, but there was something he had to see to first. And it was going to be a pleasure.

There was no shortage of combustibles; the place was brimming with old newspapers and rags. It probably meant something to someone, at one time, but now it was all junk – or rather, fuel.

He began his revenge calmly, but excitement swiftly took over. His movements became frantic and jerky, as he dashed around the rooms on the first landing, scattering anything flammable around the floor, then downstairs; systematically going from room to room, taking great pleasure in each tiny twinkling flame that burst from every match he struck. As the flames took hold, he started to laugh. *He'd show the bitch. No one gets the better of Vincent Webb. No one.*

Despite the damp of the old furnishings, they began to smoulder. Little crackling flames burst into life, eating up the curtains, and then, the old sofa. Vincent watched with glee, as the flames sputtered and spread, and thick black smoke began to fill up the house.

Vincent laughed, as he backed towards the door. "Burn, baby, burn."

The stench of smoke was like an aphrodisiac. He wanted to stay and watch, to hear them screaming. He wanted to see them burn. But, self-preservation told him to get well away. He might even stop down the road, and watch from a distance. *Yeah, that's what he'd do.* He'd watch the whole damn place go up in smoke, see the flames licking through the roof, and know that the fire had got them.

With one last look around, he pulled on his leather trench coat, picked up the holdalls, and left the smouldering, blistering house. He sauntered over to the car he'd stolen last night, whistling to himself. His head still throbbed, but it didn't matter now. He'd got her. She was about to pay. She was as good as dead.

With Nash out of the picture, whatever he got for this lot was his, and his alone. He'd be set up for life. He'd invest it; let it make money for him. He'd go abroad, maybe California, for the hell of it. See it, for his old mate. He chuckled to himself. *What a joke.* He was glad Nash was dead – more than glad; he was delighted.

He threw the holdalls into the boot of the car, and slid into the driver's seat. The car was less than a year old, a beauty. It would start. Not like that other heap of junk. He almost had the key in the ignition, when he saw what had been done.

At first, he couldn't comprehend it. The wiring was hanging out of the dashboard; the gauges smashed. Vandalised, wrecked, unusable.

He felt like his head was going to explode. Confusion swamped him. "What the…" Then, it dawned on him. "Nash! The cretin must have done this before trying to attack me upstairs." Slumping back in the driver's seat, Vincent could almost see that ugly, twisted face jeering at him.

Slamming his fist down on the dashboard, making another dial jump out, he threw back his head, and roared, "I'm not beaten yet. Do you hear me! You haven't beaten me yet."

Chapter 29

Ian was sweating and shivering, all at the same time. His gut felt like it had been twisted into a knot, and his thoughts were a mess of guilt, disbelief and terror. He tried to block out the images flashing through his head of his wife and daughter. His thoughts were driving him insane. *Dear God, where were they?*

The police were still swarming around Benjamin's house and garden, knocking at neighbours' doors, asking questions. They'd wanted to know what Julia and Lucy's blood types were. Grimes had said it was routine, but he wasn't stupid. They'd clearly found blood which may not have been the old man's.

He'd phoned Steph last night, hoping against hope to hear Julia's voice on the line, but it was her sister, who'd gone practically hysterical when he told her what had happened. She'd wanted to race straight round, but he stopped her. There was nothing she could do here. Better if she stayed put – in case Julia was okay. In case they turned up.

Possibly, they'd gone somewhere else; they hadn't got caught up with someone who'd murdered their neighbour. They'd turn up at Steph's later today, and wonder what all the fuss was about.

But, he couldn't sit here and wait any longer. Just getting in his car and driving – searching would be better than that. This was the worst, this waiting and staring at the clock was making him go crazy with worry.

He grabbed his coat and car keys, and slammed the front door behind him. As he turned the ignition key, O'Ryan came across the road, and stopped him. Ian rolled down the side window.

"I can't sit, and do nothing," Ian blurted out. "At least if I'm looking…"

O'Ryan remained calm. "I understand how you must be feeling, Mr. Logan, but you'll gain nothing by driving aimlessly. If there's any news, we'll hear it first."

Ian closed his eyes, and leant his forehead on the steering wheel. "What's happened to them, Inspector? Where are they?"

O'Ryan shook his head. "I wish I had the answer, but we'll hear something before long. Forensics haven't come back with definite results yet about the other vehicle. But we're checking on stolen vehicles, particularly dark blue ones. It's top priority, Mr. Logan."

Why hadn't they given it top priority twenty-hour hours ago, instead of trying to pin the crime on him? He wanted to yell at them, but there was no point. Besides, this was his fault entirely. If he hadn't messed around with another woman, Julia wouldn't have been forced to leave him.

"Chief!"

Ian and O'Ryan spun around to see Grimes running towards them.

"Sir, we've got something."

Ian shot out of the car. "What? What have you got?"

"It came through on the radio. A fisherman out at the reservoir spotted some tyre tracks leading straight into the water. He waded in, seems he's got those big rubber waders, and he says there's definitely a submerged vehicle. There's a tow truck heading there now, sir."

"Julia's Mini?" Ian asked, although he dreaded hearing the answer.

Grimes looked awkwardly at him. "We don't know yet, sir."

"Right, let's move it," O'Ryan said, striding off towards a police car. "Reservoir's only about five miles away."

"I'll follow," Ian said, starting his car.

O'Ryan stopped in his tracks. "That's not such a good idea, Mr. Logan. It might be better if you stayed put. We don't know what we're going to find."

"I'm coming," Ian snapped.

The officers made no more argument, and Ian followed the police car, with its sirens wailing and blue lights flashing. O'Ryan could certainly drive, Ian realised as he tailed him, praying the car wasn't Julia's. It had been years since he prayed, and now, he chanted our all those childhood prayers like a mantra.

Maybe the police didn't know what to expect, but he feared the worst, and as they sped round the winding country lanes, he'd half hoped he'd lose control, and smash himself into a tree so he could be reunited with his family, without first having to undergo the nightmare which lay ahead.

Within minutes, they had screamed to a halt at the side of the reservoir. A tow truck was preparing to back towards the water's edge. Two police frogmen were already in the bleak grey water.

Ian's courage failed him. He knew he ought to be in the water now, reaching for them. But, he couldn't. He couldn't face seeing them dead. *Not Lucy. Dear God, not his little girl.*

O'Ryan came over to him; his face was grave. "It might be better if you waited in the car, sir. This might be very disturbing for you."

But, Ian was looking at the tyre tracks in the mud, and his despair lifted fractionally, faintly aware he was glad that the crazy drive here hadn't resulted in him killing himself. "The tracks…" He got out of his car, his eyes fixed on the tracks.

"Please stay in the car Mr. Logan," stressed O'Ryan.

Ian turned to him, positive now. "No, it's alright. Look, don't you see?"

"I'm not with you, sir."

"They aren't Julia's," Ian exclaimed, suddenly elated. "The wheel base is too wide for her old Mini. And the tread is nothing like hers."

"Actually, you're right. That's a bigger car altogether, and I'd say those tyres are pretty bald." O'Ryan's face melted into sympathy. "I hope you're right, Mr. Logan, I truly do."

Silently, they stood, watching the frogmen attach the hook to the submerged vehicle. Slowly, the winch turned. Ian's moment of jubilation fragmented into terror. His family could be in the car. They could have got rid of the witnesses and the car in one go, then, taken Julia's Mini. It made sense. He stood, trembling, as gradually, a car was dragged up onto the muddy slope, water pouring from every orifice; a dark blue Renault.

Pre-empting he was about to run and open the car door, O'Ryan grabbed his arm, holding him back. "Hang on, sir. Let the boys do their checking first. It's for the best, believe me."

Ian stood there, mute, terrified of what they might find. When it was on dry land, an officer opened the driver's door, and jumped aside, as brown water gushed out all over his feet. Another officer opened the boot. There was something in there, but not bodies. His knees buckled. "Thank God."

The windscreen was cracked, and there was a dent and a broken indicator light.

"Couple of suitcases, sir," an officer called out. "Want me to open them?"

Ian wandered bleakly to where the officer stood holding the sodden suitcases. They were the ones they'd taken to Devon earlier that year. The look on his face was all O'Ryan needed. The hand on Ian's shoulder was no comfort at all.

Chapter 30

"Smoke!" Julia screamed. She could smell the awful stench. She clutched Lucy to her, passing on this new terror to her daughter. Oh, what wouldn't she give to deliver her child from this nightmare. She would willingly suffer a hundred times over, if only Lucy were safe.

"Smoke... Mummy!" Lucy's voice rose in panic. "Mummy, something's burning!"

Releasing her, Julia balanced along the floor beam to the window, and peered out. Wisps of grey smoke were spiralling upwards. "Oh my God," she murmured. "Oh my God." Far below, she saw the car Vincent had returned with was still parked near her Mini. *So, he was still here.*

But, surely, he wasn't still lurking on the next landing, forcing them out by setting fire to the building She thought she'd heard him downstairs, moving about. No one in their right mind would remain behind in a burning house. However, Vincent was not in his right mind.

"We have to get out, Lucy. Now. Through this window." She grabbed what was left of the chair. "Don't look, Lucy. I'm going to smash it, and make a hole for us to climb through. Turn your head away, darling."

"Mummy, I'm frightened."

"It's okay, sweetheart..." She took aim. Using all the strength she possessed, she smashed the chair through the window. The glass shattered easily, and Julia banged away at the rotting wood framework and shards of glass, until there was a clear hole to squeeze through. Cold air swept in, bringing with it the acrid stench of smoke. "Lucy, we have to be very brave now."

The child's face was ashen and solemn, but her blue eyes were wide and full of trust. She nodded.

Helping her daughter to the window, Julia went first. Squeezing through the tiny hole, her eyes locked onto her daughter's terrified face, as she lowered herself onto the sloping roof five feet below. To her horror, she could feel the heat from the blaze through the roof tiles. Out here in the open, she could hear the crackling, and the roaring of the fire, as the flames took hold. Her eyes smarted, as choking black and grey billows of smoke swept past, forming a great ugly pillar in the white sky.

Doubts filled her head. *Would they have been better off trying to get down the stairs?* Although, judging by the amount of smoke, the lower floors must be well ablaze by now. They'd had no choice. Steadying herself on the sloping apex, she held up her arms to Lucy, who was standing at the broken window. "Come to me, darling. It's perfectly safe. Lucy, please…"

"I can't!" the child cried, stricken rigid with fear. "We're too high. We'll fall off the roof."

"Lucy, you must," Julia pleaded.

"I can't!" she wailed, sobbing hysterically now.

It broke Julia's heart to be strict now, but it was the only way. Sternly, she snapped, "Lucy Logan, you do as you're told right this minute, or…"

The child disappeared. She vanished from the window back into the attic.

Julia's heart lurched. "Lucy!" she screamed, trying desperately to scramble back up the wall and though the window. "Lucy!" But, she couldn't hoist herself up. There was nothing to lever herself up on, she didn't have the strength. "Lucy, get back here, Lucy!"

The little girl's face suddenly reappeared, and Julia crumpled with relief. "Oh God, Lucy, you gave me such a fright."

"I forgot Mister Brown," the child explained, wiping her eyes, and tucking the teddy inside her jumper, as she scrambled out of the window.

Balancing precariously, Julia reached upwards to her daughter, hauling her through the hole, and into the safety of her arms. She gripped her fiercely, terrified in case she slipped and fell.

Lucy's face was smudged with tears. "Mummy, it's hot."

"I know, darling," Julia murmured, getting her balance, trying to acclimatise herself to the predicament. She felt as if they were perched on the edge of the world. Looking down at the sheer drop, her head began to spin. Great gusts of smoke spiralled upwards, choking and blinding. Her eyes stung cruelly.

"I can't see any way down," she breathed wretchedly.

"We could climb down that drainpipe," Lucy suggested.

Julia looked to where her daughter was pointing. There was a drainpipe leading from the gutter down to the main roof, then down to the ground. But, whether it would hold them, she didn't know. Yet, she couldn't see any other way down.

Between clouds of billowing black smoke, Julia glimpsed fields. There was a farmer and his dog rounding up sheep. At first, the sight made her want to weep, and then, in desperation, she shouted at the top of her voice. Lucy joined in, both coughing and spluttering, as the wind fanned the smoke into their faces. Finally, the intense heat warned them there was no time to lose. If the flames had taken hold of the bedrooms, then, the lower roof could cave in at any moment. This was their one and only chance.

She gasped out instructions to Lucy. "We're going to slowly slide on our bottoms down this little roof to the drainpipe. Then you're going to climb down first…"

"No!"

"I'm not arguing, Lucy Logan, listen, and do as I say. You're light, so it will hold your weight. Mummy's heavier, so I'll follow after you."

Gripping Lucy's wrist, they inched down the slope where Julia explained how she was to tackle the drainpipe. "You'll skin your knees, darling, but cling to it with your hands and feet, like a little monkey." She tried to smile. "You can do it darling, I know you can."

As soon as Lucy gripped the drainpipe, she instantly let go. "It's hot!"

"I know, sweetheart. Be brave, please."

"You follow straight away, Mummy," Lucy begged, entwining her little arms and legs around the pipe, as best she could. "You're not really very heavy."

"As soon as you're down. Go quickly, now!"

For all her tender years, Julia admired her daughter. She was asking more than any mother should ask her child, and it broke her heart to expect her to even try and do this. But, without another word, Lucy turned onto her stomach, and lowered herself, feet first down onto the drainpipe. Julia kept a hold of her daughter's arm, until she had descended beyond her reach.

"Try to hold your breath when the smoke gets too thick," Julia called. "And keep your eyes closed. Think nice thoughts, don't be frightened. You can do it, sweetheart. I know you can."

The child made no reply, her concentration fixed on her task. Julia's heart swelled with pride.

Smoke was pouring up through the bedroom windows now, and the heat through the tiles was becoming unbearable. Lucy's progress was painfully slow, and Julia tried to keep up a steady stream of words of encouragement.

She was probably ten feet below her, when Lucy peered up fearfully. "Mummy, the pipe is so hot."

"Don't let go! Lucy, you mustn't let go. Keep climbing down. You can do it. Only please hurry, love."

"It's burning my hands!" Lucy screamed. "I can't hold on… Mummy, help me!"

"I'm coming!" Julia cried, swinging her legs over the apex, clinging to the pipe and guttering, realising then what a task she'd set her daughter. It was scalding hot, and so close to the wall, almost impossible to grip.

Somehow, she shimmied downwards, half expecting the pipe to peel away from the wall with her added weight. Whether they could survive a fall from this height, she had no idea, but she could feel the flames roaring upwards. The whole house pulsated with the heat.

She slid more than climbed down the pipe, feeling the skin being torn off her knees, as she scraped past scalding hot bricks. When her feet were close to Lucy's head, she cried out, "Grab my legs, Lucy. Wrap yourself around my legs. Put me between you and the pipe, I'll lower us both."

Lucy was sobbing and screaming, but Julia suddenly felt the weight of the child, as she managed to grab one leg and then the other, dragging her down. It was almost unbearable. Only her determination stopped her from giving in to the pain. There was no way she could ease herself slowly. She slid agonisingly fast, the rough metal of the pipe ripping and burning the skin from her hands.

She sensed the ground rushing up to meet them. Tree branches were suddenly on a level, then above her, flames were leaping out from windows, heat was scorching her hair, her eyes. And then Lucy's weight eased as she hit the ground, followed by Julia a second later, landing half on top of her daughter on the blackened grass.

At that second, Julia was barely aware of the pain. All that mattered was making sure Lucy was alive. Scrambling off her, she brushed her hair back, staring frantically down into her blacked face. Through the smoky grime, her mouth curved, and the tiniest of smiles transformed her face.

Hauling her to her feet, they staggered away from the house, into a clearing where the air was less putrid. They failed to see arms outstretched. Blinded by the smoke and their own watery vision, they saw no one, until they had stumbled straight into him.

Chapter 31

The dark blue Renault was winched onto the tow truck, and taken away for forensic investigation. A team of policemen, some with dogs, descended on the area, and began a search. Ian watched. He felt sick. They were searching for bodies. No one had to tell him that. The murdering bastards had dumped their car here, and taken Julia's. No way would they have taken them along for the ride. It was logical. They'd killed once, two more deaths wouldn't make much difference. Covering their tracks, leaving no one to point the finger.

He felt numb. All feeling, all sensation seemed to be draining from his body and his mind, preparing him for the shock. *Nature's way*, he supposed.

Chief Inspector O'Ryan came over, he regarded Ian pitifully. "You may as well go home, Mr. Logan. There's nothing here. We'll keep you informed of progress."

"I'm not going anywhere," he blurted out, anger erupting suddenly and unexpectedly, lashing out as O'Ryan tried to console him. "I'm going to help in the search. If Julia and my daughter are here, I'll find them."

"Sir…"

He shoved the officer aside, and stumbled off into the woods, giving way to tears spilling down his face. Blindly, he forged through the undergrowth, his hands and clothing snaring on the bracken. His heart lurched at every mound of dead leaves he came upon. He was vaguely aware of Grimes on his tail, telling him the police had it all in hand, and he might be doing more harm than good; they had tracker dogs at work here. They were going to have to drag him away by force, if they wanted him to stop now.

He stumbled on, wanting to die, wanting the earth to open up and claim him. They were gone, dead...

"Mr. Logan!"

"Leave me alone!" he yelled back at O'Ryan.

"Mr. Logan!" he shouted again, louder.

Glancing back, Ian saw the officer running towards him, looking bulky and ungainly. He felt his stomach tighten. This was it. They'd found something... his family...

But, as O'Ryan drew nearer, he saw the officer's expression. The man looked almost excited.

"What?" Ian uttered, terrified, exulted, daring for a second to hope. "What is it?"

"Reports coming in about a house fire four miles away, old derelict place. No one's lived there for years."

"Meaning?"

"The farmer who reported the blaze also reported he thought he saw two people on the roof. He thought it might be a woman and a child."

Ian didn't wait to hear any more. He ran back to the parked cars. "Which way?" he yelled, as they tore through the bracken. "Which way, for God's sake?"

"Grimes has the engine running. Get in with us," O'Ryan said breathlessly.

Ian threw himself into the rear seat of the police car. It was already screeching off, as O'Ryan jumped into the passenger seat.

Sirens blaring, Grimes took off, scattering police officers in all directions. Ian sat perched on the edge of his seat, hanging over the driver's shoulder, his foot hard down on his own invisible accelerator pedal, willing them to go faster.

"They were on the roof?" he demanded, hanging onto the seat back as they were flung in all directions. "When? How long since the report came in?"

"A few minutes. The fire service is on the scene."

"What sort of house is it—a bungalow? What?"

"Big pre-war type, I think," Grimes answered, as he squealed the vehicle around a sharp bend, sending both passengers hard against the side of the car. "Sorry!"

Ian's brain was spinning. *What were they doing on the roof? And how the hell could his little girl get down off a roof, without killing herself for God's sake? How could Julia? She was no good at climbing.* "Can't you go any faster?"

Grimes could. Slamming the car up a gear causing the engine to protest, Grimes put his foot hard down on the accelerator, throwing his passengers into the backs of their seats. The outside world flashed by in a vague greenish-brown blur.

"Look!" O'Ryan suddenly yelled. "Smoke above those trees."

Ian saw the great pall of black smoke hanging in the air like a gigantic gravestone. His blood ran cold. The acrid stench of smoke drifted in through the car's heater vents, and as they grew nearer, the sound of fire engine horns drowned out everything else.

Three fire engines had squeezed up the narrow lane ahead of them, and another came roaring around the bend behind them. Grimes pulled the car onto a grass verge, and Ian was out of the car, before it had barely stopped. Running, he ducked past the fire officer, who tried to bar his way. What did stop him in his tracks was the sight he was suddenly faced with.

The house, probably quite impressive in its day, stood there, a pitiful burnt out blackened shell. Firemen were hosing water in through the windows. The heat scorched his skin, even from where he stood. The air was thick and choking with vile stinging smoke. He glanced up at the roof. This was where Julia and Lucy had been spotted. There was nothing left of the roof, save a few charred, blackened beams, still smouldering. Otherwise, the house gaped obscenely up at the black sky.

His legs moved automatically, drawing him closer to the charred shell. There was no urgency now. This was where they had ended their lives, then, this place.

Something on the black charred ground caught his eye. His legs took him towards it, and he stooped down. A small battered teddy bear lay there, blackened by the smoke. He picked it up, and cradled it against his heart.

"You've found it, then?" someone said.

Ian turned slowly. There was a man in thick clothing and wellingtons. He was smiling. "What did you say?"

He pointed to the teddy. "You've found it? Mister Brown, the little girl's teddy. She was making a right song and dance about not having the darn thing when they loaded her into the ambulance."

"Ambulance?" Ian gasped, launching himself at the man, grabbing him by the shoulders. "You saw her? She's alright? She's alive?"

"And kicking! And her mam…"

"Where are they? Where did they go?" Ian begged, almost shaking the information out of the man.

"City Hospital, I reckon. I was the one that raised the alarm," he added, already starting to recount the tale that would earn him a couple of beers in the local pub for many a night to come. "I was out in the fields tending the flock, when Nipper, that's my dog, got the scent of the smoke, and started barking like crazy. I turned round, and saw the old place going up in smoke. You could have knocked me down with a feather when I saw the two of them up on the roof, shouting and waving."

"And they got down alright?" Ian urged, half laughing, half crying. He beckoned Chief Inspector O'Ryan over to them. "They're alive! They've been taken to the City Hospital. This is the chap who called it in."

The farmer continued his yarn. "Got myself over here pretty smartish, after I'd called the fire people, and blow me down, the pair of them were shimmying down the drainpipe like a couple of trapeze artists. Straight into my arms they came, black as the ace of spades, and a bit worse for wear, but they'd made it."

Ian hugged the man. "I'll come back to you – only I've got to get to the hospital. Will you take me, Inspector?"

O'Ryan's face broke into a beaming smile. "Mr. Logan, it will be my greatest pleasure."

Chapter 32

Julia was desperate for a cup of tea and some pain killers, but soon discovered there was protocol to contend with at the hospital. They'd wanted to separate her and Lucy and bring in some child specialist but there was no way she was letting Lucy out of her sight. They'd had to get out of their clothing, which had all been bagged up. Now they sat in white paper overalls waiting for the police to come and take a statement.

Despite the pain and everything she'd gone through, Lucy was smiling. Julia's heart swelled with admiration and love, overjoyed she could at last look into her daughter's face and not see terror in her eyes.

When the door to their private room opened, Julia jumped, fearful that it was him – Vincent, but the two men who walked in were every inch police officers. The shorter one in a sheepskin coat introduced himself as Chief Inspector O'Ryan, and his colleague was Detective Inspector Grimes.

She wondered where Ian was. *Would he come? Was he concerned or had he been having the time of his life with his mistress?* Her heart lurched and she blinked back a rush of tears.

"Mrs. Julia Logan?"

She nodded.

The officer who had spoken said nothing for a moment, as if he was just letting that piece of information sink in. And then, in a subdued voice said, "I'm sure you'd rather be having a cup of tea and getting those injuries tended. But we need to talk to you, and get a statement."

"Does my husband know I'm here?"

"He's outside," O'Ryan said, then smiled slightly. "He's desperate to see you both."

"Practically had to cuff him to a chair," the younger officer joked, smiling broadly.

She was glad Ian wasn't allowed in yet. She wasn't ready to face him.

She took a deep breath. "There were two of them." She waited for the officer to take out his notebook, before continuing. She spoke slowly, so he could get the facts written. "Nash was in his early twenties, and badly disfigured. He had a scar down his cheek. I think he's dead. You'll probably find his remains in the house, near the stairs."

"And the other one?" O'Ryan asked softly.

Julia shuddered. "I think the other one got away. He wasn't stupid enough to start a fire he couldn't get well away from. She levelled her gaze at the police officer. "His name was Vincent. He was about six feet tall, broad shouldered, blond hair, good looking, pale blue eyes." She shuddered again. "Cold eyes, and I hope to God you find his body in the ashes, too, but I don't think you will."

Two nurses took Lucy off into another room, and Julie re-lived the nightmare for the police officers, surprising herself and them at how calmly she could talk about it. Except when it came to telling them about being raped. Relating what that vile individual had done, made her sick, but at least, he hadn't touched Lucy.

O'Ryan spoke gently. "I'll arrange for someone to come and talk to you. We have a rape counselling service. It might help."

She shook her head. "I'd rather just go home."

But first came a physical examination with the doctor taking swabs. Eventually they dealt with her injuries.

When they brought Lucy back into her she was clutching her teddy. "Daddy found Mister Brown!"

Ian followed Lucy into the room. He looked exhausted, pale and un-shaven. His ashen face crumpled when he saw her. He stumbled forward, falling to his knees at her feet, his head in her lap, sobbing. "Thank God you've alive. Thank God! I thought I'd lost you both." He drew Lucy into his embrace. "I'm so sorry."

"Don't cry, Daddy."

Julia sat mutely, bandaged arms hanging limply at her sides. He gazed up into her face, his eyes creased in pain. "Oh, God, what did they do to you?"

She couldn't speak, couldn't even begin to try and explain to him. She shifted her focus to O'Ryan. "Can we go home now?"

The Chief nodded. "I'll drive you."

Chapter 33

They drove in silence, his wife and daughter clutching each other's hands, not saying a word. Maybe, once Lucy was tucked up in bed, Julia would open up and talk to him, but he wouldn't push her. She would tell him, in her own good time.

She needed to know about his affair. He still had to face that. But, for now, all that mattered was they were alive, and he had them safely back. He was never going to risk losing them again.

Turning into their street, Julia gasped at the sight of their neighbour's house cordoned off by police tape. She hadn't asked the police officers what crime they'd committed. She'd guessed. And now she knew.

"Poor Benjamin," she whispered. "Is he...?"

Ian nodded slightly, wanting to shield his daughter from the evil of this world, and then realised he'd already failed miserably in that.

"And Bess?"

Detective Inspector Grimes answered. "Hanging on in there."

They said nothing else, and when O'Ryan pulled up outside the house, Ian got out, carrying Lucy indoors, his other arm around his wife.

"We'll speak tomorrow, Mrs. Logan," said O'Ryan. "Try and get a good night's sleep."

Closing the door on the night's cold air, Ian carried Lucy upstairs. "I'll run you both a bath."

Julia followed him upstairs and stood with her arms around Lucy as he turned on the taps and poured scented lotions into the water, working up a lather. He had to peel Lucy out of the overall his daughter had been put in, then lowered her gently into the warm water.

"Try and keep your hands dry, or your dressings will come off. Does it hurt very much?"

"No. I'm okay. But Mummy hurts. That horrible man made her nose bleed."

Ian looked back at her, standing in the doorway, despising himself for letting her down, for putting her through this. "I'm so sorry," he mouthed.

She turned away.

With Lucy's hair washed, and the smoke and grime all cleansed away, he dressed his daughter in pyjamas and tucked her into bed. "Hot chocolate?"

She beamed a smile at him. "And chocolate biscuits? I'm starving. Oh, and will you wash Mister Brown. He's too mucky to get in my bed."

"I will indeed." He kissed her forehead. "I'll be back in a few minutes."

When he came downstairs, Julia was rooting through a kitchen drawer, her movements awkward with her hands all bandaged. He longed to take her in his arms. "Julia..."

"I need plastic bags," she snapped, holding up her hands. "I can't get these wet, only I can't grip anything..."

"I'll find something."

"I can do it!"

"Sweetheart, let me..."

She slammed the drawer shut. "I can manage! I've managed well enough with those two maniacs, I'm sure I'm capable of finding two plastic bags in my own kitchen!" Her voice broke on a sob and her shoulders hunched.

His arms went around her, pulling her close. She was trembling, and even though her eyelids were squeezed shut, tears forced their way through her lashes. Words tumbled from her lips, coming out in huge distraught sobs. "Oh Ian, I never thought I'd see home again. I thought we were going to die. I thought we'd be m... murdered. He told Nash to finish us off, only he couldn't, so he hid us in the attic, and because of that, he ended up dead instead. They fought, and there was this awful crash when the stairs gave way, and he died."

Ian led her into the lounge, settled her onto the sofa and sat close, his arms tightly around her. Between sobs she described the horrendous place where she'd been held captive, and all the while, he'd been here, whining on about the rotten time he was having.

"He raped me, Ian. The worst one, Vincent. And he hit me... hurt me."

"Sweet Jesus," Ian groaned, wishing he could close his ears, as she told him everything. He listened in misery, despising himself. Loving her more than life itself. When she was all talked out, he held her close, cradling her in his arms, rocking her gently.

She needed to bathe, and he ran a bath for her. He wanted to ask if he could help sponge her back, wash her hair. But she said she'd manage. Whether she would ever allow any intimacies ever again, he didn't know. He closed the bathroom door, went downstairs and made hot chocolate for Lucy.

Lucy was asleep before Julia came back downstairs. He made food for her, and sat watching her as she ate. She said no more about her ordeal. The silence made him wonder if it was his cue to admit to his affair.

"You know how sorry..." he began, but she stopped him.

"I don't want to hear. Not now... not yet." She got to her feet. "I'm tired, Ian. I'll go to bed."

With her settled, he rang Steph, who broke into sobs of relief when she heard they were safely back. She promised to come around in the morning.

Julia was fast asleep when he slid between the sheets. He lay close to her, breathing in her scent, his arm across her waist. But he couldn't sleep. Torturous images were running through his head. He wanted to kill the heinous bastard who had done this to his family. Hopefully, they would find two bodies in the ashes. He would ring O'Ryan first thing and find out.

When he did eventually sleep, he slept like a log, and awoke to find Julia's side of the bed empty. Panic seized him, until he heard her downstairs. The radio was on, and he could hear her moving about. Moments later, Lucy shuffled into his room and climbed into bed beside him. He cuddled her. "How's your hands and knees, sweetie?"

"A bit sore. Where's Mummy?"

"Downstairs. Come on, let's go and have breakfast. Are you hungry?"

"Starving. Did you wash Mister Brown?"

"I'll do that after breakfast."

She chuckled. "Shall we peg him out on the line to dry."

"Good idea," he smiled, marvelling at her powers of recovery. At least he hoped she was on the mend. The physical injuries would heal. It was the scars on her mind that worried him most – and on Julia's, too.

Lucy brought an armful of toys downstairs with her, which were soon scattered around the living room. In the kitchen, Julia was struggling to set out the breakfast things with her hands bandaged.

She smiled at him and his heart turned over. "It's like wearing boxing gloves. I can't do anything."

"I'm sorry for putting you through all this. If I hadn't been such a blasted fool…"

"I know." She looked earnestly at him. "Are you still seeing her?"

"No. I ended it the night you left me. I'm a fool. I've no excuses. I hope you'll forgive me. I understand if you can't."

She didn't answer, but continued trying to make breakfast.

"Let me do that," he offered, putting spoons by bowls.

"I'll get dressed – if I can find anything to wear…" her voice trailed off.

"We'll go clothes shopping, as soon as you're up to it."

"Lucy's going to need a new school uniform too."

"It's only clothes. You're what matters. You're safe now."

She went to go upstairs, but stopped by the kitchen door, looking at the crack in the glass. "What happened?"

"I was a bit frantic and frustrated when the police were putting the blame on me."

"For what? For Benjamin?" she asked, aghast.

"It's sorted now."

"We'll have to get it fixed."

"Yes."

She stood in the doorway. "Will you speak to the police today, ask them, Ian. Ask how many bodies they found in the house."

"I will."

"And ask about Bessie. See how she is."

He smiled. It was wonderful to have his family back.

Chief Inspector O'Ryan was the second caller of the morning. Stephanie was the first, arriving as they were finishing breakfast. She listened in horrified silence as to what they'd gone through. When the police arrived, she took Lucy off into the garden.

"How are you feeling?" O'Ryan asked, addressing the question to the both of them, although Ian guessed it was Julia he actually cared about.

To his surprise and delight, she slid her arm through his. "Recovering."

Ian covered her hand with his own.

"I'm glad to hear that." O'Ryan glanced out of the window. "Who's the woman with your daughter?"

"My sister, Stephanie," Julia answered.

O'Ryan nodded. "She's an amazing little girl. There's help, you know, if she starts having nightmares or flashbacks – and that goes for the both of you."

Ignoring his offer, Julia asked sharply, "How many bodies did you find?"

He hesitated before answering. "Just the one. Michael Nash. Dental records have confirmed who he was. He'd had a lot of dental treatment, after getting his face badly gashed. A nasty piece of work. He'd done a bit of time. Seems he had a real chip on his shoulder, because of his appearance. A violent so-and-so, by all accounts."

"He saved our lives," said Julia softly. "That's what the fight was about. He hid us in the attic, and told Vincent he'd killed us and buried us. *He* was the worst one—Vincent. That man has no compassion, no mercy."

"And that's why we need to find him," said the Inspector. "We will get him, have no fear. In fact, one of my reasons for calling round is to ask if you could come into the station, and look through some pictures. Later this afternoon would be good. See if you can identify this Vincent character."

"Yes, he needs to be found, locked up..." her voice trailed away, and Ian felt her shudder.

"Also, I'm afraid your car probably won't be back with you this side of Christmas. Our men are going over it, but it needs to stay impounded, until everything is sorted."

"I don't want it back!" Julia said sharply. She turned to Ian. "I don't! I never want to see it again. Please, Inspector, get rid of it."

Ian squeezed his wife's hand. "I'll see to it, sweetheart. We won't bring it back here, I promise."

"And the other thing I needed to speak to you about, Mrs. Logan," said O'Ryan, "is to ask you to accompany me to your neighbour's house, and see if you can help us sort out what's been taken. I would appreciate it if we could do that as soon as possible. Now, if you could."

"I'll try," agreed Julia. "I know he kept a record of his valuables. Insurance purposes, I imagine. There'll be photographs on his computer. He may have been old, but he was on the ball with technology."

"That will come in very useful. If we have a list of items that might suddenly come onto the market, then we may catch our man a lot quicker."

Julia eased her arm free from Ian's. "I'll get my coat. Ian, don't let Lucy out of your sight."

"She's only in the garden with Steph. She's fine, sweetheart."

"But, he's still out there – that Vincent," she said, her voice rising. "We're still witnesses. Have you forgotten that?"

"He's not going to come back here," Ian promised. But, the moment Julia got her coat and went out to speak to her sister and Lucy, O'Ryan stepped a little closer to him.

"Your wife is right, Mr. Logan. Be on your guard. Vigilant at all times. He will be running scared now, and he's got nothing to lose. With his partner dead, he's going to cop for everything – the murder, the robbery, the kidnapping. Your wife is a vital witness. It's possible he might try and make sure she can't testify against him in court."

Ian's heart sank. He'd thought the nightmare was over, but the way the Inspector was speaking, it may well only just have begun.

While Julia was with O'Ryan over at Benjamin's house, he took a steadying breath, and rang his boss at work. He couldn't go back there; it wasn't fair on Shelley. God only knew how they'd manage without his salary; he hoped Julia would understand.

The first thing he had to do when Tony Wyndham came on the line was to apologise for lying about his absence from work. He babbled on, talking quickly about what had gone on; about Julia and Lucy; about the neighbour being killed; about his affair with Shelley; about the fact the murder would be in the papers; about resigning.

When he finally ran out of words, there was a long silence on the other end of the phone, before Tony spoke. "Bloody hell, Ian. You don't do things by halves, do you!"

They talked some more, with Ian answering the barrage of questions that came flying his way once Tony had got over the initial shock.

"It will probably be all over the papers," Tony added.

"Hopefully, the Press won't have picked up on my wife and daughter's kidnapping."

"And you think resigning from your job is going to help them?"

"Well, no but..."

"Exactly! You're going nowhere. We need you here."

"It's not fair on Shelley..."

"We'll sort something. For now, you look after that family of yours, Ian. Take a couple of weeks off. Get yourself, and them, sorted, okay?"

Ian finally put the phone down, feeling a huge weight had been lifted from his shoulders. They needed the police to put a name to the murdering bastard who kidnapped and raped his wife, and life would be back on track.

Chapter 34

Shelley de Main read the newspaper story with morbid curiosity. Stories were always more interesting when you knew the people involved personally. Not that she'd ever met Benjamin Stanton, but he lived, or *had* lived, on the same road as Ian, and according to the papers, his wife did the old man's shopping. The entire incident was quite a saga – headline news.

She folded the paper, and slipped it into her bag. She'd read it in more detail once she got to work. She needed to go in, although she doubted Ian would make an appearance. The place would be buzzing with talk. Roger hadn't wanted her to go into work, thinking she was too upset after being attacked. At one point, he'd even hinted at her attacker being linked to this burglary. How right he was, but she dismissed his suggestion out of hand.

As she guessed, the office was in an uproar. Everyone was talking about the murder of Ian Logan's neighbour, and there were now stories filtering out about his wife and daughter being involved, somehow. She joined in the debate; subtly hinting about how strange it was Ian hadn't been in work these last few days. He could be more involved than the papers were saying. As she joined in with the gossip, she didn't actually say *arrested,* but she enjoyed splattering the mud about, in the hope some would stick.

She wasn't surprised to be called into the managing director's office later that morning. He was probably eager to know what was being said, but he could hardly be seen to be out there gossiping.

Tony Wyndham indicated the leather chair near his desk. "Please sit down, Shelley."

She sat, looking steadily at him, eager to continue the assassination of Ian Logan's character. Tony was quite attractive in a stocky sort of way, a little thin on top, but didn't that denote a man's virility. Or was that a fallacy put about by balding men. It might be interesting to find out.

He leaned back in his chair, fingers entwined, a questioning look in his eyes. "Shelley, I gather you've read the papers—this awful murder that's happened on Ian's street."

She cut him off in mid-sentence. "It makes you wonder, doesn't it? And the fact he's not in work..."

Tony reined back. "Hold on. Ian's not at work, because he's got some personal issues. I'm not sure how long he'll be off – until he's sorted, simple as that."

She avoided his stare. *Typical the boys all stick together.* She wondered how much he knew. Ian had hinted about resigning. *Well, it didn't look that way now.* For a moment, she wasn't sure whether that pleased her, or not. Although there was no way she'd allow him to crawl back into her bed, after what he'd done. She took a deep breath. "*Was* he involved with the murder? You know I've always thought he was too perfect to be true."

"No," Tony Wyndham said, flatly. "He has some personal issues – you being one of them."

She felt her cheeks colouring. "What are you talking about?"

"He rang me yesterday, wanting to hand in his notice. Basically, Shelley, I know about the two of you, and it's clear you can't work in close proximity, so better all-round if we moved you to the sub-branch..."

"Moved *me*!"

"No change in pay."

Her mouth fell open. "Are you serious? Ian Logan is probably involved in this *to-do* right up to his neck. Why the hell didn't you accept his resignation?"

He leant forward across his desk, his voice low. "Because he's good at his job, and I don't want to lose him. Plus, he's already been through hell."

"*He's* been through hell?"

"He has, and I'm not adding to his problems." He got to his feet. "Well, that's all for now. Take this week to get your move sorted. You'll be fine. You can recover the additional fuel costs on expenses."

Her cheeks were flaming, and her thoughts spinning. There was no point arguing. She would have to tell Roger this move to the sub-branch was promotion. But, she was going to find some other way of making Mr. Perfect Ian Logan suffer.

As she left the office, with Tony Wyndham's words ringing in her ears, she decided Mr. Perfect Logan would not get away scot-free. Perhaps a call on his wife one of these days would do the trick. She smiled to herself. Yes, a visit to Julia Logan would make her feel much better.

It had taken three hours of searching police records to come up with the name of the man who had raped his wife, Vincent Webb. Ian had stood with his arms around Julia, staring at the face on the screen, despising it.

Over the following days, things had moved quickly. A car had been reported stolen a few miles from the house where they'd held Julia and Lucy. It went missing the evening before the fire. The police assumed Webb had nicked it.

Shortly after that, the stolen car had been found dumped in a multi-storey car park in Birmingham. Sightings of Vincent Webb came in by the bucketful—mainly in the Birmingham area, although some reports came in from London and even some in Glasgow.

The best news they heard the following week was a London antiques dealer had been arrested for handling stolen goods, and amongst the hoard the police found, were items matching those owned by Benjamin Stanton.

To give O'Ryan his due, he called round to their house to report on progress regularly. "So, we know Vincent Webb has money in his pocket," he'd said, two days ago. "It's my guess he'll be looking to get out of the country now, but we're watching the ports and airports. We will get him!"

"I wish he *was* out of the country," Julia had said. "As far away from here as possible."

"The net is closing in on him, Mrs. Logan. We'll have him before much longer, you can count on it," promised the confident Inspector.

Chapter 35

Julia stood at the front door, and watched Ian set off for work. It wasn't until his car had turned out of the drive, wheels crunching on the frost, she felt the first tingle of panic. Having him at home for the past three weeks had been good for both of them. They'd found time to talk, and he'd answered all her questions about his affair. Even when it would have been less painful not to have known the details, she had asked, and he had answered – truthfully.

It hadn't come as a shock to learn he'd been seeing a woman from work, although it had shocked her to learn how she'd gone at him with a pair of scissors.

She'd been surprised, too, to discover he'd handed in his resignation, and more than relieved his boss hadn't accepted it.

Watching him drive off to work now made her stomach tighten. *What if Shelley de Main was still mad at him? Was she liable to try and stab him again? What if she crept up behind him, when he was at his desk? What if she got his jugular, instead of his hand, the next time?* She should have warned him.

Feeling hot and panicked, she went back inside, closing the door, leaning against it, and struggling to get her imagination back under control. Shelley de Main wasn't a cold-blooded killer. There was only one of those about. And there was still no news of Vincent Webb being arrested.

Before going back into the kitchen to prepare Lucy's breakfast and school packed lunch, she hesitated. Turning, she slid the safety chain across the door. Moments later, Lucy bounded down the stairs. She was so lovely in her new school uniform, and so normal. It was a big day for all of them. Ian was back at work, and Lucy was back in school.

After breakfast, Julia wrapped her daughter – and herself—up snugly in scarves, gloves, and woolly hats, before setting out for school.

It was wonderful to be back in the old routine, and good to meet up with the other mums, who were all desperate to know how she was after the ordeal, which was now common knowledge. Although she hadn't let it be known she was raped, no doubt that would come out in the trial, if Vincent Webb was ever caught, but, for now, it was secret from everyone, except those closest to her.

She did a little shopping before going home. Things they needed, she told herself. Not an excuse to delay going into an empty house. When she did turn the key, and close the door on the outside world, slipping the safety chain on again, she stopped, eyes darting around the hall. Everything was exactly as she'd left it two hours ago. But, an uncomfortable silence greeted her, except for the whirring and ticking of the clock.

Her heart was beating much too fast, but she took off her coat and outdoor clothing, hung it up, switched on the TV for background noise – and for news, and made a start on the housework. The injuries from climbing down a scalding drainpipe were healing fast. Cumbersome bandages were now a thing of the past.

Oddly, she enjoyed getting to grips with the chores. The dust had built up over the last few weeks, and she was glad to see the surfaces starting to shine again. She was thinking about what to cook for their evening meal, when the shrill ringing of the phone made her jump. Annoyed with herself for being so jumpy, she picked up the receiver.

No one spoke, and the silence was so loud she could hear the clock ticking again. There was another sound, however—a faint sound of breathing. Someone was there. Her skin crawled.

Slamming the phone down, she stood, heart thudding, then, snatching it up again, she dialled the number which would tell her who her last caller was. Not surprisingly, she discovered the caller had withheld their number.

Somehow, she got through the day, but she was on edge. Leaving home to pick up Lucy from school had her looking up and down Sycamore Drive, before setting out on foot. Then, she walked swiftly, checking over her shoulder time and again.

Only when they had eaten, and Lucy was tucked up in bed, did she tell Ian of her fears.

"It doesn't mean anything, sweetheart," Ian said convincingly "It was probably a wrong number, or a fault on the line."

"It was him," Julia breathed. "It was Vincent Webb. I know it."

"Julia, don't do this," Ian said, holding her. "If you start to think every little thing is down to him, you'll drive yourself crazy."

"They haven't found him yet, though, Ian. It could have been him."

"Why would it be?" Ian said softly. "He'll be too afraid to make contact. He doesn't know the police aren't keeping a trace on our calls. He won't want to give them any leads, that's for sure. And, why would he, anyway?"

She wanted to believe him. However, she was petrified he would come for her. He wasn't the sort to let anyone get one up on him. And she had. She had got herself and Lucy away from them. She doubted he would let that lie.

The following day, she double-checked the doors and windows, before taking Lucy to school. She walked briskly, holding her daughter's hand tightly, giving alleyways and isolated areas a wide birth, and quickening her pace whenever a car slowed. She was alert, her eyes and ears sharp. At the school gates, she scanned the faces, afraid he would be there, biding his time.

Lucy's class teacher was on playground duty. Spotting her, she came over, smiling. "It's so good to have Lucy back safe and sound. How are you? That was a terrible ordeal for you both."

"We… we're fine, getting back to normal," Julia said, trying to smile, trying to stop her eyes from darting this way and that. "The police haven't caught the man…"

"I heard," said the teacher kindly.

"I'm worrying unnecessarily, I know…"

The teacher touched her hand. "Lucy is safe here, Mrs. Logan. No one will touch her. You can be sure of that."

She sounded so confident, and walking home from school, Julia prayed the teacher was right.

Back at home, she made herself a coffee, and tried to relax and do all the things she used to do, but she jumped at every sound. Even her reflected shadow in the glass of the kitchen door set her heart pounding. Unable to settle, she rang Chief Inspector O'Ryan on the direct number she'd been given. He was out, but Len Grimes took her call.

"Mrs. Logan, how are you? I'm afraid we've still no news yet. I imagine that's why you're ringing."

Her hopes plummeted. "Oh! I was hoping you'd found and arrested him…"

"You would be the first to know," he said kindly. "But, I'm sorry, no concrete news so far. Plenty of sightings—we're exploring a possible lead in the Dover area. Fingers crossed."

"Yes," she murmured. "Fingers crossed."

She hung up, and tried to concentrate on all the mundane everyday tasks she once did without a second thought. Making beds, doing the laundry, preparing something nice for dinner, but all the while, she felt nervous, uneasy, as if she was being watched. She could practically feel those pale cold eyes leering at her from every corner. And then, taking out the rubbish, Julia saw him.

At the bottom of her garden was a hedge, and beyond that, was a narrow track and open fields. It had been their main reason for buying this house. And that was where she saw him – walking along behind the hedge. He hadn't looked her way, but she had glimpsed the shoulders of his black leather coat, and saw his arrogant profile and that blond hair.

Stunned, gulping back her scream, she tore back into the kitchen, slamming the door, shooting the bolt across. She was shaking so badly she couldn't dial the police's number. It took three attempts, and then, it was an eternity before someone answered.

"Grimes here..."

For a second, she couldn't speak, and then the words came tumbling out. "I've seen him. He's here! Vincent Webb. I saw him over the top of my hedge. He's here!"

"On our way!" Grimes yelled. "Stay indoors, keep the doors and windows locked. Someone will be right with you."

"Hurry!" Julia begged, still gripping the receiver, her back pressed hard to the wall, breathing hard, expecting him to burst through a door or window at any second.

A stream of police cars pulled up in the street, sirens screaming. In no time, the entire area was cordoned off, and police, some with dogs, were swarming everywhere. Someone must have fetched Ian, because his car came hurtling down the road, minutes after the police.

But, there was no sign of Vincent Webb.

Nothing.

"I thought it was him," Julia murmured much later, when nothing had materialised, and she was left feeling idiotic.

"It's perfectly alright, Mrs. Logan," said Chief Inspector O'Ryan. "Far better to be on your guard, although I honestly can't see him showing his face around here. He must know every copper in the land is on to him."

Julia rested her head on Ian's shoulder. "I feel so stupid, panicking like that."

"Shall I ring Steph?" Ian asked gently. "Get her to come and stay with you for a while?"

"No! I don't need a babysitter," Julia snapped. "Oh, Ian, I'm sorry. I know you're only trying to help. Go back to work. I'll be fine, honestly."

Reluctantly, he eventually returned to work, and gradually, the police dispersed. Julia tried not to be on edge when she went to fetch Lucy from school, but walking back, a fog came down, reminding her of that awful night when it had happened.

Gripping Lucy's hand so tightly the child complained, they walked quickly back from school, their clipped footsteps echoing uncannily through the darkness.

Memories were racing through her mind. Thoughts of how she had sat waiting for Ian to come home. How she had loaded her suitcases in her car, and then, taken Lucy from her bed. It hurt, knowing at that moment poor Benjamin had been lying dead – or dying. By the time they reached home, she felt sick with fear. She locked the door, and put the chain on. Relieved to be back home, and with the curtains drawn, the television on, and dinner cooking, she began to relax a little. The ringing of the front doorbell, a short while before Ian was due home, shattered the mood.

Lucy came rushing into the kitchen. "Someone's at the door. Don't answer it, Mummy!"

The bell chimed again, insistent, as if someone was keeping their finger pressed firmly on the button, determined not to be ignored. Julia, held her daughter close, her feet riveted to the floor. But, the ringing went on.

"It might be those policemen," Lucy whispered, but her wide eyes hinted at who she feared it was.

Julia's hatred for Vincent Webb overshadowed her fear right at that moment. *How dare he terrorise her child and her in this way?* But, it could be the police. Maybe they'd come to tell her they'd arrested him. She crept to the window and drew the curtains aside a fraction. The fog had thickened, but Julia could distinctly see a woman standing at the door. She wore a hooded coat, not dissimilar to her own winter's coat. Curiosity took the place of fear.

"It's a woman!"

"He might be in disguise," Lucy fretted, hanging onto her arm.

"No, she's too small. She's about my height." Irritated with being frightened of her own shadow practically, she went to the door, nevertheless keeping the door on the security chain, as she inched it open. "Yes?"

The woman glared steadily at her from beneath the fur brim of her hood. She wore too much eye make-up, was Julia's first thought.

"My name is Shelley de Main," the woman introduced herself, her face half obscured by the fur-edged hood of her coat. "Your husband may have mentioned me, but probably not. We need to talk."

Julia felt her legs weaken, as she stared into the plump face, the red lipstick, everything accentuated about this woman who Ian had risked everything for. Her first instinct was to slam the door in her face. Instead, she reassured Lucy, who was hovering close by. "Go back and watch your program, sweetheart. Everything's okay. It's a woman from daddy's work."

She waited until Lucy had gone back into the lounge. "Yes, he's mentioned you. What do you want?"

"To talk. Perhaps you weren't aware we've been seeing each other."

"I know all about it," Julia uttered, trying not to show her pain. It was one thing Ian confessing to an affair, but another to be confronted with the woman he'd had sex with.

Shelley de Main's mouth gaped, like someone had stolen her thunder, and her voice went up an octave. "I wonder if he's told you we've been lovers for months. And that we'd have sex practically every lunchtime?"

Julia had heard enough, she moved to shut the door, only to feel the woman's foot against it.

"And you know all the times he was working late, well, that would be when we'd take a drive out, and make love in the back of his car. Your child's booster seat would get in the way someti…"

"Move your foot, or I'll slam this door, and snap your ankle in two," Julia said, gritting her teeth.

Shelley didn't move. Except for her mouth that curved into a sultry kind of smile, mocking her. "So what's it like being married to a man who cheats on his wife at every opportunity? Does your little girl know what sort of man her daddy is?"

"Mummy?" Lucy was there, behind her. Her voice was a whimper. "Make her go away."

"I'm warning you," Julia said, moving Lucy back a little. "Go upstairs, sweetheart."

Shelley was shouting now. "No, don't go, kid. Did you know your precious daddy…."

Julia moved swiftly, jerking the chain from the door, she opened the door wider, then slammed it hard against Shelley's ankle. The woman shrieked with pain, and stumbled backwards. She had no chance to say more. Julia slammed the door shut, leant hard on it, and found herself looking straight into Lucy's troubled eyes.

Her chin trembled. "Why doesn't she like my daddy?"

"She's a grumpy, cross lady." She pressed a kiss to the top of Lucy's head. "She's gone. Good riddance. Forget she was ever here, darling. I'm not going to give her another thought." And she meant it.

Chapter 36

Ian drove home from work slowly, the fog was hampering progress, and the headlights of approaching cars came and went like ghostly spotlights. There had been no more frantic phone calls, no more panics. Life would eventually return to normal. He would have to be patient. It was understandable Julia couldn't feel totally safe again. It would take time, and it certainly wouldn't happen before Vincent Webb was behind bars.

He sighed. That was going to be another ordeal for his wife, re-living the whole terrifying nightmare in court. If there was some way he could deliver her from that, he would.

He turned into his street, slowing to swing onto his drive, and that was when he spotted something on the pavement. A dark shadowy mound lying there. He stamped on the brakes, quickened the speed of his windscreen wipers to try and get a clearer view. A person. Someone lying there.

"Dear God!"

He sprang out of the car, leaving the engine running. Then, as if he'd been punched in the gut he skidded to a stop, recognising the coat first, the hooded camel coloured coat, Julia's coat. It was the new one he'd bought her since her own was destroyed along with the other things she'd packed to leave him. Things that had ended up in the reservoir.

"Julia!" He threw himself down beside the unmoving form. A puddle of blood was oozing out from inside hood. "No," he uttered. "No, no no…"

He reached out to pull the hood back, to see her face, so see if she was breathing.

Shelley de Main was unconscious on his path.

"It's too much of a coincidence!" Julia said, over and over again – to him, to the police, to everyone.

"Sweetheart," Ian tried to console her. "Vincent Webb has nothing to do with this attack. Love, you're starting to become paranoid. Every time the phone rings, every time you see a blond-haired man. You've got to get things into proportion. Shelley de Main got herself mugged; it happens. You heard what O'Ryan said. Webb has been spotted on the south coast. He's possibly looking for a boat to get across to Europe. He can't be in two places at once."

"Ian, you're wrong!" Julia screamed. "Shelley de Main looked like me in that coat. You even said so yourself. She'd come from our house. He must have been watching, and thought it was me."

Ian took her hands in his, giving her a little shake. "He isn't watching the house. He isn't going to hurt you again. Love, it's been weeks now. It's over. You have to try and forget. When Shelley de Main recovers consciousness…"

"If!"

"*When* she does," Ian insisted. "She'll be able to identify her attacker. O'Ryan is putting a police officer by her bedside, so the minute she comes around, we'll know."

Julia rested her head against his chest. "I'm frightened, Ian. I'm really frightened."

"Don't be!" he ordered. "Vincent Webb is long gone. He'd be a fool to come back to this area, now, wouldn't he?"

And, at that moment, he honestly believed he was right.

Chapter 37

Lucy awoke from her dream with a start. Her head was hot, and her heart was thumping. The nightmares always made her feel like this. She clambered out of bed, and switched on the bedroom light. Curling back under the covers, she searched for Mister Brown, and whispered in his ear, "It's okay, Mister Brown, dreams can't hurt us."

The nightmares came less often now. At first, she had wanted to run into her parents' room, but that would remind Mummy about it all again, and she didn't want that to happen. She wanted her mummy to forget all about it, like she was trying to do.

Downstairs, she heard the chinking of milk bottles, which told her it would be soon time to get up. She decided then to get dressed early. Today was very special. Today was the school nativity play – and she was going to be an angel.

Shelley de Main's dark rimmed eyes flickered open. Smells of disinfectant invaded her senses. Slowly, she moved her head on the pillow, as she tried to focus on the room. A get well soon card stood on top of a pale wooden cabinet. It was daylight, but a blanket of grey fog was all she could see through the hospital window.

A policeman sat in a chair opposite her. His eyes were shut. She tried to speak; her voice was feeble, barely audible even to her own ears. It was enough to stir him though. He looked at her, then jumped to his feet. He pressed a button above her head, and dragged his chair closer to her. He seemed too young to be a policeman, just a boy.

"How are you feeling, Mrs. De Main?"

She pulled a face.

He smiled. "Do you remember what happened to you?"

Shelley didn't try to speak at first, but allowed the images in her head to sort themselves out. A malicious little thought struck her. She could tell this policeman it was Ian Logan, or his idiotic wife, who had smashed her skull in. The prospect of seeing them trying to squirm out of that brought a faint smile to her lips.

A nurse came in, and took her pulse.

"Do you recall anything, Mrs. De Main, anything at all?" the baby-faced policeman asked softly. "We want to catch the person who did this to you."

"He hit me from behind," Shelley murmured. "I remember lying on the pavement and looking up at him. I must have blacked out then, but what I do remember is thinking what a handsome man he was. Under different circumstances, I could have taken a fancy to him."

The policeman took out a notebook. "Could you describe him?"

She tried to ignore the pain in her head. She would let Ian Logan off the hook. He'd have an alibi, anyway. She concentrated on the man hovering over her, and the expression on his face. It was almost as if he was puzzled at the sight of her. As if she wasn't the person he expected her to be. And then, he'd gone.

Her throat felt parched, as she said, "He was tall and blond, and he wore a black leather trench coat, with silver buttons." She tried to smile at the policeman; he really was rather cute. "Anybody you know?"

"You were wonderful!" Julia exclaimed, as Lucy scrambled off the school stage, and ran to her parents at the end of the nativity play.

The audience of rapt mothers, fathers, and grandparents were all congratulating their talented offspring, as the children were allowed to mingle with them, before being herded back into class.

Lucy was radiant in her angel's gown, and sparkling wings and halo. But, the thing that brought tears to Julia's eyes was the look on her little girl's face, as if the last threads of the nightmare were gone forever.

"You were brilliant!" Ian added, hugging her. "You outshone everyone."

"We're having a party in our classroom," Lucy said excitedly. "Miss has brought cakes and fizzy pop."

"Lovely," Julia smiled, trying not to think about Shelley de Main being hit over the head, right outside her house last night. She was desperate to know if she had regained consciousness. Hopefully, she hadn't died. Surely, they would have heard from the police if she'd died. She hugged her daughter, forced a smile. "Have a wonderful time, Lucy, sweetheart. Have fun."

The teacher clapped her hands to round up her class. With a final kiss for her parents, Lucy skipped back to join her classmates. Ian squeezed Julia's hand. "Time to go."

She nodded, getting up, and waving to the line of children making their way out of the hall. In the doorway, Lucy turned, hesitated, and then, ran back to give her mummy one last kiss.

Ian laughed. "Come, love. I'll run you back home, and then, get into work."

With her arm through his, they left the warmth of the school, and stepped out into the fog. She shivered. "I hate the fog, Ian. Take care driving, won't you?"

"I will," he promised, kissing her, "and I'll be home early. No more late nights, I promise."

"I know," she murmured, trusting him, loving him.

The drive home was slow, the swirling fog making progress almost impossible. Eventually, they reached Sycamore Drive. Julia kissed Ian again, as she got out of the car.

"Will you be alright?" Ian asked. "You're not going to fret and worry over what happened last night. The two things aren't connected."

"Don't worry. I'll be fine. Drive carefully."

As he drove away, Julia went indoors, glad to be out of the icy cold fog. She hated the smell and the feel of it, hated the way it isolated you.

The state of the lounge and hall made her stop in her tracks. She shook her head. Lucy had got up early, and with time on her hands, had managed to get about every toy she possessed out to play with, even her doll's house, which she'd brought downstairs, only to leave in the hall. With a sigh, she set about her first chore of tidying up before she tripped and broke her neck.

Gathering up all the little things first, and loaded with as much as she could carry, she went upstairs, and deposited the toys in Lucy's toy box, then picked up last nights discarded dungarees to hang in the wardrobe.

Pulling open the wardrobe door, the smell of leather swept out. Thick black leather filling her nostrils, swarming through her head, chilling the blood in her veins.

Heart stopping, she slammed the wardrobe door on the smell, her skin crawling with terror. But, a force – an invisible force from the inside of the wardrobe, pushed against her. The door flew open. And out stepped a nightmare.

Vincent Webb stood there, smiling. Wide, pale, insane eyes glittered, as brightly as the long-bladed knife in his hand.

A choking sensation swelled up in her throat, stopping her from screaming. But, her limbs still obeyed her, and she turned and fled from the room, pulling the door shut after her. Racing down the stairs, her feet skidded on the carpet. Her spine bumped against three steps, before she was back on her feet, terror numbing any sensations of pain. She reached the front door, cursing herself for putting the safety chain on, but then a long vicious blade was slammed against her hand, burying itself into the wood, skimming the skin from her finger.

He towered over her, smelling of leather and sweat. Cold, pale eyes filled with loathing and anger. She brought her knee up into his groin as hard as she could. It wasn't hard enough, she knew that, but in the second he took to wince, she was under his arm, leaping Lucy's doll's house like a hurdle. The kitchen held some sort of defence – knives, pans, and the back door – escape. But, it was locked, double-bolted to keep him out. The irony of it made her sob. Reaching the kitchen, she heard his yell, as he tripped over the doll's house, and stumbled headlong at her.

With all her might, she slammed the glass door in his face.

The top of his skull hit the cracked glass panel, and his blond head smashed clean through it. She raced to the back door. It had been prised open. She flung it wide, glancing swiftly over her shoulder to see where he was. Far off in the distance, she could hear police sirens wailing. *You're too late*, she screaming inside her skull. Within two seconds, she would feel that blade.

But, she saw he was on his knees, his head sticking through a hole in the glass door. Jagged pieces of patterned glass littered the kitchen floor, other pieces jutted up towards his throat. A triangular slither hung above his neck. The needle-sharp points were already sticking into his skin, trickles of blood dripping onto her floor.

He didn't move, couldn't move. To move meant forcing the glass deeper into his flesh, into his veins. He turned his merciless pale eyes up to her, wide with terror. "Help me," he pleaded.

Julia could feel her heart pounding in her chest. She stood mesmerised. Now, he wasn't so terrifying. He looked pathetic, stuck there, too afraid to move, begging her to have mercy on him.

As the police sirens grew louder, her thoughts flew back to the terror he'd put her and Lucy through, even to the diabolical way he'd treated Nash. And now, he wanted mercy.

"Please..."

She spoke calmly, so he understood. "You murdered a harmless old man." She walked slowly towards him, her eyes fixed on his. Wanting him to see she was no longer afraid. "You tried to kill his dog. Bessie survived, you know. She's well again, and has a new home. Not that you care. You care about nothing, and no one, do you? You even killed your own accomplice."

"Need ambulance," he uttered, not able to form the words properly, as that would entail moving the muscles in his throat, and shards of glass were already pressing against his jugular.

"Yes, you do," she agreed, standing over him. She touched the top of his blond head, as if she cared.

The sirens were closer now, probably at the end of the street.

She placed both of her hands on the top of his head, confident in what she intended doing. Because, really, there was only one thing she could do.

She pressed down slowly, so he knew.

His feet skidded frantically against the hall flooring, his fingers clawing at the door from the other side of the glass. "No!" he screamed. "I'm sorry, okay. I'm sorry."

Julia eased back on the pressure on his head. She spoke softly, without emotion. "That's good. I'm glad you're sorry. But, frankly, Vincent, it's far too late."

And with one downward thrust, she rammed his throat hard down onto the shards of glass.

A gargling sound blubbered from Vincent Webb's mouth.

Outside the sirens wailed to silence. Car doors slammed. She wondered vaguely how the police knew. She would ask them later. But, for now, she walked calmly towards her back door. Once more, she turned around. A pool of dark red was spreading across her kitchen floor.

Quietly and confidently, she stepped outside into the fog.

THE END